The
TORTILLA FACTORY

The TORTILLA FACTORY

Gary Paulsen

PAINTINGS BY

Ruth Wright Paulsen

Harcourt Brace & Company

SAN DIEGO NEW YORK LONDON

Text copyright © 1995 by Gary Paulsen
Illustrations copyright © 1995 by Ruth Wright Paulsen

Requests for permission to make copies of any part of
the work should be mailed to: Permissions Department,
Harcourt Brace & Company, 6277 Sea Harbor Drive,
Orlando, Florida 32887-6777.

Library of Congress Cataloging-in-Publication Data
Paulsen, Gary.
The tortilla factory / by Gary Paulsen;
illustrated by Ruth Wright Paulsen.—1st ed.
p.   cm.
ISBN 0-15-292876-6
1. Tortillas—Juvenile literature.
[1. Tortillas.]   I. Paulsen, Ruth, ill. II. Title.
TX770.T65P38   1995
641.8'2–DC20   93-48590

PRINTED IN SINGAPORE

First edition
A B C D E

...Through Your goodness we have this bread to offer,
Which earth has given and human hands have made.
It will become for us the bread of life.
—The Sacramentary of the Roman Missal

The black earth sleeps in winter.

But in the spring the black earth
is worked by brown hands

that plant yellow seeds,

which become green plants rustling in soft wind

and make golden corn to dry in
hot sun and be ground into flour

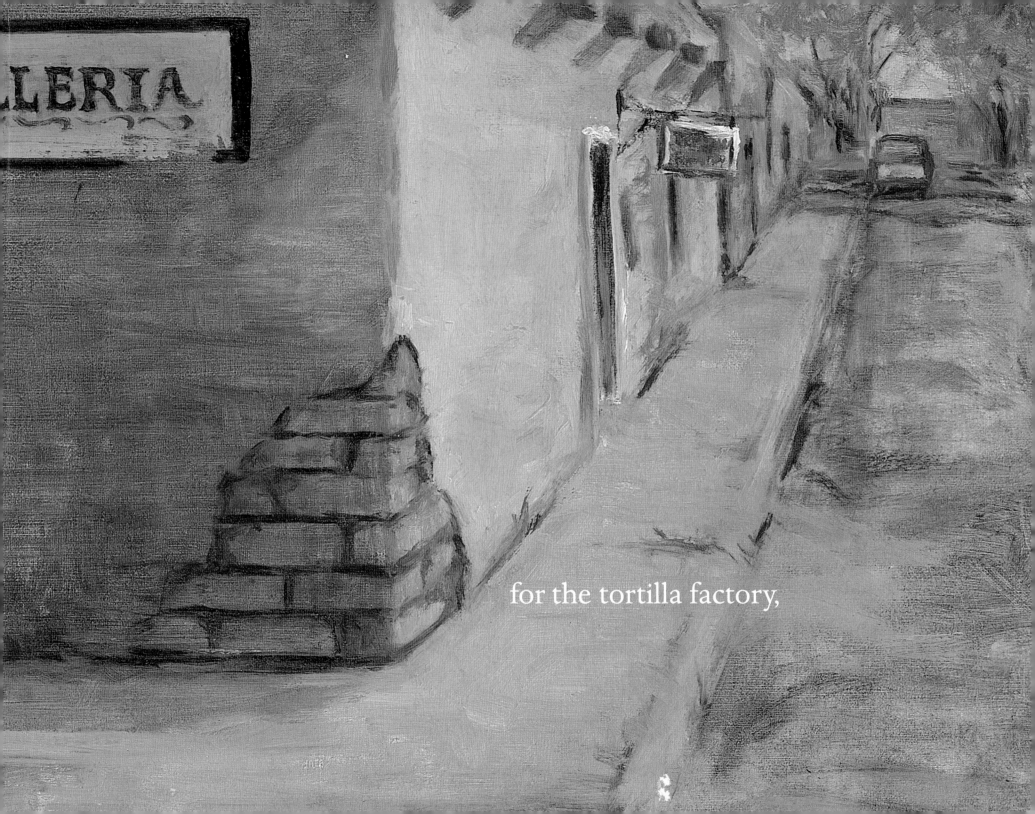

for the tortilla factory,

where laughing people and clank-clunking
machinery mix the flour into dough,

and push the dough,
and squeeze the dough,
and flatten the dough…

Lemon-Ricotta Cheesecake

———◆———

Make the cheesecake the night before the barbecue, and remove it from the refrigerator just before serving.

2½ cups gingersnap cookie crumbs (about 40 cookies)

½ cup margarine or butter, melted

2 containers (15 ounces each) ricotta cheese

½ cup sugar

½ cup milk

2 teaspoons vanilla

4 eggs

Lemon Topping (right)

Heat oven to 325°. Mix together cookie crumbs and margarine; press on bottom and side of springform pan, 10 × 3 inches. Place ricotta cheese in blender or food processor; cover and blend or process until smooth. Stir in remaining ingredients except Lemon Topping. Pour mixture into pan. Bake 1 hour to 1 hour and 15 minutes or until cheesecake is set in center. Let cool. Spoon Lemon Topping over cheesecake and refrigerate at least 4 hours but no longer than 48 hours.

Lemon Topping

⅔ cup water

⅓ cup lemon juice

⅓ cup sugar

1 tablespoon cornstarch

1 tablespoon grated lemon peel

Mix all ingredients in small saucepan. Cook over low heat, 2 to 4 minutes, stirring frequently, until mixture is thick. Cool slightly before spooning over cheesecake.

Spring Tea

Stilton Cheese Biscuits*

Orange-Currant Scones*

Chocolate-Hazelnut Torte*

Lemon Curd Tarts*

Tea*

Tea Sandwiches*

Serves 10

A little something in the late afternoon is always appealing, no doubt the reason that tea parties are so welcome. A tea party is also a lovely way to visit with friends, as virtually all the cooking is done before the party begins. Guests can pour their own tea, so you are free to chat; all you need to do during the party is keep an eye on the teapot, refilling it when necessary, and refill plates of food when they run low. A tea party is an appealing way to celebrate your grandmother's birthday (she and her friends won't be out late), honor a visiting guest who is booked for lunch and dinner or celebrate an engagement informally. While tea is often considered a feminine ritual, it's quite all right to invite men—they will enjoy the delicious goodies every bit as much.

THE FINISHING TOUCH

◆ Use your prettiest vase—both crystal and silver are excellent choices—and fill it almost to overflowing with such lovely spring flowers as tulips, iris and lily of the valley (roses are delightful too). Use flowers in any combination or alone, whatever suits your table and your budget.

◆ This is the time to pull out an heirloom lace, embroidered or crocheted tablecloth. If you don't have such a tablecloth, a simple white cloth will also work nicely.

◆ Set out cloth napkins that work well with your tablecloth. White napkins are a good choice, even with a white tablecloth.

✦ Indulge yourself and buy a pretty teapot that you may have had your eye on. Or use your favorite teapot—china, ceramic or silver. You'll want at least two teapots, so you don't have to keep running to the kitchen, but they don't have to match.

✦ Bring out your prettiest china, serving plates and platters. You may want to ask friends or family if you can borrow a few pieces that coordinate with your serving dishes, to make an attractive table.

✦ Place china plates, a teapot and silverware at each end of your table. In between, arrange plates and platters of food. This allows more than one guest at a time to serve themselves.

✦ Round up as many small tables as possible and place them next to chairs and sofas so your guests will have plenty of room to put down plates and teacups.

✦ Include family or friends in preparing tea sandwiches and passing food. Children especially enjoy helping out and feeling "grown up."

✦ Make a pot of "flavored" tea—apricot, raspberry, apple cinnamon—for children and guests who don't drink caffeinated tea.

✦ Make your own tea invitations by picking pansies about three weeks before the party. Place the flowers between two pieces of brown paper and weight them with a heavy book or two for a week. For each invitation, glue a single pressed pansy to the upper corner of a sheet of plain white notepaper.

Stilton Cheese Biscuits

---✦---

You'll find cheese easier to shred when it's cold.

½ cup shortening

2 cups all-purpose flour

2 teaspoons sugar

3 teaspoons baking powder

¼ teaspoon salt

1 cup milk

½ cup shredded Stilton or Cheddar cheese

Heat oven to 450°. Cut shortening into flour, sugar, baking powder and salt in large bowl with pastry blender until mixture resembles fine crumbs. Stir in milk and cheese until dough leaves side of bowl. Drop by tablespoonfuls onto greased cookie sheet. Bake 10 to 12 minutes until golden brown. Immediately remove from cookie sheet. *1 dozen biscuits.*

A homemade pansy invitation (see above) announces tea time when placed in a straw hat trimmed with dried flowers.

Following pages: *Spring Tea set out for guests.*

Tea Time

Orange-Currant Scones

◆

½ cup currants

⅓ cup margarine or butter

1¾ cups all-purpose flour

3 tablespoons sugar

2½ teaspoons baking powder

¼ teaspoon salt

1 tablespoon grated orange peel

1 egg, beaten

4 to 6 tablespoons half-and-half

1 egg white, beaten

Heat oven to 400°. Soak currants in warm water for 10 minutes to soften; drain. Cut margarine into flour, sugar, baking powder and salt with pastry blender until mixture resembles fine crumbs. Stir in orange peel, egg, currants and just enough half-and-half until dough leaves side of bowl.

Turn dough onto lightly floured surface. Knead lightly 10 times. Divide dough into 2 parts. Roll or pat into two 6-inch circles about ½ inch thick. Place on ungreased cookie sheet; brush with beaten egg white. Bake 10 to 12 minutes or until golden brown. Immediately remove from cookie sheet. Cut into wedges to serve.

About 20 scones.

Orange-Currant Scones served with marmalade.

Chocolate Hazelnut Torte

Chocolate Hazelnut Torte

———————— ◆ ————————

Save time by preparing this stunning torte a day ahead; it keeps well covered in the refrigerator. Grind the nuts ¼ cup at a time to keep them from getting too oily.

> *6 ounces sweet cooking chocolate*
>
> *¾ cup margarine or butter*
>
> *4 eggs, separated*
>
> *⅛ teaspoon salt*
>
> *¾ cup sugar*
>
> *¾ cup ground hazelnuts*
>
> *2 tablespoons hazelnut liqueur or 2 table-*
> *spoons coffee*
>
> *Hazelnuts*

Heat oven to 375°. Grease and flour springform pan, 8 × 2½ inches. Heat chocolate and margarine in medium saucepan until melted; cool 5 minutes.

Beat egg whites and salt in medium bowl on high speed until stiff. Beat egg yolks and sugar on medium speed until lemon colored; stir into chocolate mixture. Stir in ground hazelnuts and liqueur. Gently fold chocolate mixture into egg whites; pour into pan.

Bake 40 to 45 minutes until top is dry and knife inserted in center comes out slightly wet. Cool completely; remove from pan. Garnish with whole hazelnuts.

Lemon Curd Tarts

———— ✦ ————

These pretty tarts can be made the day before the party. Just cover tightly and refrigerate.

Pecan Tart Shells (below)
1 teaspoon unflavored gelatin
1 tablespoon cold water
½ cup sugar
2 eggs
2 tablespoons grated lemon peel
¼ cup lemon juice
2 tablespoons margarine or butter

Prepare Pecan Tart Shells; cool. Sprinkle gelatin on cold water in medium saucepan to soften. Beat sugar and eggs until thick and lemon colored; stir into gelatin mixture. Heat just to boiling over low heat, stirring constantly, about 15 minutes. Remove from heat; stir in lemon peel, lemon juice and margarine. Pour lemon mixture into Pecan Tart Shells. Refrigerate 1 hour until set.

24 tarts.

Pecan Tart Shells

1 cup all-purpose flour
½ cup finely chopped pecans
¼ cup sugar
¼ cup margarine or butter
1 egg

Heat oven to 375°. Mix flour, pecans and sugar; blend in margarine and egg until crumbly. Press in bottom and up side of ungreased small-muffin cups, 1¾ × 1 inch. Bake 10 to 12 minutes until light golden brown. Cool tart shells in pan.

TEA

Follow these tips for a perfect pot of tea.

- ✦ Use fresh, cold tap water.
- ✦ Select good-quality tea.
- ✦ Don't use an aluminum pot.
- ✦ Warm the pot with hot water before brewing tea.
- ✦ If using a tea ball or infuser, don't pack tea tightly.
- ✦ If using loose tea, measure 1 teaspoon per cup plus 1 teaspoon for the pot.
- ✦ Bring water to a full rolling boil before adding it to the tea.
- ✦ Let tea steep for about 5 minutes. Strain loose tea or remove tea ball.
- ✦ Stir tea before serving.

A tea set just for children helps include them in the party.

Tea Sandwiches

—————◆—————

10 slices thin white bread
10 slices thin pumpernickel bread
10 slices thin whole wheat bread
Sandwich Fillings (below)

Cut crusts off bread; cut bread into shapes using cookie cutters, or cut each square into 4 triangles or squares. Spread bread with choice of fillings; cover bread with plastic wrap. Garnish sandwiches with parsley, watercress and violets if desired. Cover sandwiches tightly and refrigerate until ready to serve.

30 sandwiches.

Cucumber Filling

Unsalted margarine or butter
1 large cucumber, pared and thinly sliced

Spread white bread with margarine; top with slices of cucumber.

Cream Cheese and Watercress Filling

1 package (3 ounces) cream cheese, softened
1 small bunch fresh watercress, finely chopped

Mix cream cheese and watercress in small bowl. Spread pumpernickel bread with cream cheese mixture.

Orange-Currant Scones (upper left), *assorted Tea Sandwiches* (middle) *and Lemon Curd Tarts* (upper right).

Deviled Ham Filling

1½ cups finely chopped fully cooked smoked ham
¼ cup finely chopped parsley
3 tablespoons mayonnaise
1 tablespoon Dijon mustard

Mix all ingredients in small bowl. Spread mixture on whole wheat bread.

Earth Day Picnic

Pocket Sandwiches*

Spring Breeze Punch*

Tabbouleh Salad*

Soft Ginger Cookies*

Serves 6

Celebrating Earth Day, April 22, is a fairly recent idea, and one that many people will want to turn into an annual tradition. It's an excellent day to enjoy nature and take stock of the things we can do to keep our planet green, healthy and productive. Create a picnic for family or friends that reflects a planet-friendly view—you'll find some suggestions below. You may want to spend part of your day on a community project to clean up a local park or get rid of trash in a stream or river. And be sure to pick up after your picnic; try to leave your picnic spot cleaner than it was when you found it.

THE FINISHING TOUCH

◆ Use a natural "found object" as an impromptu centerpiece—a piece of driftwood or a pile of pretty water-polished stones. You can use flowers, berries or leaves that have fallen, too; remember, picking them isn't in the spirit of Earth Day.

◆ Spread out your picnic on a sheet or bedspread you have retired from use, and set out pretty cloth napkins, such as black and white check. After the picnic, the tablecloth and napkins can be washed and used for other outings.

◆ Set out your picnic the old-fashioned way, with nondisposable plates. Buy a set of inexpensive plastic plates in your favorite color at a five-and-dime, and use them for all your picnics, cookouts and even simple family meals.

- ✦ Use light, nondisposable plastic glasses—they are no heavier to carry than disposable ones. Not only can they be used again and again but they won't break if dropped or smash in your picnic basket.
- ✦ Bring your everyday tableware to use at the picnic, but leave fancy serving pieces at home. Kitchen forks and spoons are handy for serving. Pack a paper or cloth bag to take home dirty tableware.
- ✦ Use a pretty thermos or cooler for the punch—both were some of the first energy savers!
- ✦ Be sure to scatter some crumbs for the birds to include them in the Earth Day celebration.

Pocket Sandwiches

1½ pounds ground beef

1 pound ground lamb

3 tablespoons chopped fresh or 1 tablespoon dried marjoram leaves

1 tablespoon chopped fresh or 1 teaspoon dried thyme leaves

½ teaspoon salt

½ teaspoon pepper

2 eggs, beaten

2 cloves garlic, mashed

1 medium onion, finely chopped

6 pita breads, split

2 tomatoes, chopped

1 medium cucumber, sliced

Yogurt Sauce (right)

Heat oven to 350°. Combine all ingredients except pita, tomatoes, cucumber and Yogurt Sauce in large bowl until well blended. Spoon into loaf pan, 9 × 5 × 3 inches. Bake 1 hour until done. Cool completely. Cut into ¼-inch slices. Prepare Yogurt Sauce.

To assemble sandwiches, separate pita bread to form pocket. Place slice of meat on pita bread; top with tomato, cucumber and Yogurt Sauce.

6 sandwiches.

Yogurt Sauce

1 cup plain yogurt

1 tablespoon olive oil

1 tablespoon lemon juice

½ teaspoon pepper

Mix all ingredients.

Spring Breeze Punch

Pour sparkling water into punch 1 hour or less before serving, otherwise punch will be flat.

2 cups cold water

1 can (6 ounces) frozen tangerine juice, thawed

1 can (6 ounces) frozen grapefruit juice, thawed

1 bottle (32 ounces) sparkling water

Combine all ingredients. Serve well chilled.

1½ quarts.

Tabbouleh Salad

———◆———

Pack tabbouleh in a chilled, wide-mouthed 2-quart thermos.

1 cup bulgur

2 cups hot water

1 cup finely chopped red onion

1 cup chopped fresh parsley

⅓ cup lemon juice

¼ cup chopped fresh mint

¼ cup olive oil

2 medium tomatoes, seeded and chopped

1 medium cucumber, pared and chopped

1 clove garlic, crushed

1 cup crumbled feta cheese

Cover bulgur with water; let stand 30 to 40 minutes until tender. Drain excess liquid. Combine bulgur with remaining ingredients except cheese in large bowl until well blended. Cover and refrigerate 1 hour. Top with cheese just before serving.

Soft Ginger Cookies

———◆———

1 cup sugar

¾ cup margarine or butter

¼ cup molasses

1 egg

2 cups all-purpose flour

2 teaspoons baking soda

1 tablespoon ground ginger

1 teaspoon ground cinnamon

¼ teaspoon salt

¼ teaspoon ground cloves

½ cup sugar

Heat oven to 375°. Mix 1 cup sugar, the margarine, molasses and egg in large bowl. Combine remaining ingredients except ½ cup sugar until mixture is well blended. Shape dough by tablespoonfuls into balls; roll in ½ cup sugar. Place on ungreased cookie sheet; flatten slightly with bottom of glass dipped in sugar. Bake 6 to 8 minutes until golden brown.

3 dozen cookies.

Early American Sunday Supper

Fried Oysters with Dipping Sauce*

Beaten Biscuits*

Snap Bean Salad*

Ginger-Wine Baked Ham*

Indian Pudding with Berries*

Serves 6

*T*raditionally, Sunday supper was served in the early afternoon or, at the latest, in the early evening. It was a time that families spent together, savoring a hearty meal, talking, telling stories and enjoying each other's company. Naps after Sunday dinner are another long-standing tradition!

    This early American dinner showcases oysters, an easy-to-gather favorite for early settlers, together with old-fashioned Beaten Biscuits and Indian Pudding. The settlers learned how to cultivate corn from Native Americans; to ground corn they added molasses as a sweetener, creating Indian Pudding, a favorite from colonial times to the present.

THE FINISHING TOUCH

♦ There are several decorating styles from early American days, such as colonial and Shaker. Pick a style you like and use an appropriate item for a centerpiece. For example, a pewter bowl filled with ivy would work well for a colonial feel, and a Shaker box with wildflowers would set that theme.

♦ Leave your tabletop bare except for a runner down the middle. Use a muslin or homespun runner, quilt squares arranged

- in a line or even a small hooked rug.
- ✦ Set the table with simple tableware, and use muslin or homespun napkins. Pewter napkin rings give a colonial look.
- ✦ Pick dishes that echo early American themes—pewter, spatterware, spongeware and creamware are all good choices.
- ✦ Prop a place card in a small potted herb plant and set at each place.
- ✦ Buy wrapping paper printed to look like old newspapers. Cut wrapping paper to the size of a note card, or the size that fits your envelopes, then fold. Write your invitation on the inside.

- ✦ Spring is when many historic houses open for the season. Visit a local historic house on Sunday afternoon, and come home for this Sunday supper. Some historic houses hold plant sales, and if you know of one, plan your dinner for the weekend of the plant sale. That way you can pick up your potted herbs just before dinner.
- ✦ Ask friends to bring brochures, maps or other information on historic houses and towns. After dinner, plan a trip to one of the historic sites.

Fried Oysters
with Dipping Sauce
—————◆—————

Vegetable oil

½ cup all-purpose flour

1 teaspoon salt

¼ teaspoon pepper

1 pint shucked fresh oysters or 2 cans (8 ounces each) oysters, drained

3 eggs, beaten

1½ cups dry unseasoned bread crumbs

Lemony Cocktail Sauce (page 78)

Heat oil (1 to 1½ inches) in Dutch oven or electric fryer to 375°. Mix flour, salt and pepper. Coat oysters with flour mixture; dip into eggs, then coat with bread crumbs. Fry in small batches 2 to 3 minutes until golden brown; drain on paper towels. Serve with Lemony Cocktail Sauce.

Planning a trip to a historic house over coffee.

Table set for dinner, showing an alternative decorating idea of intertwined flowers acting as a "runner" down the middle of the table.

Beaten Biscuits

───────◆───────

Instead of kneading dough by hand, early settlers beat biscuit dough with a hammer, mallet or iron. Our suggestion of a wooden spoon or mallet also works well. If you put the baked ham in a biscuit, you'll re-create the ham and biscuit combination first found in the southern colonies.

¼ *cup shortening*

2 *cups all-purpose flour*

2 *teaspoons sugar*

½ *teaspoon salt*

¼ *teaspoon baking powder*

¾ *to 1 cup cold water*

Heat oven to 400°. Cut shortening into flour, sugar, salt and baking powder with pastry blender in large bowl until mixture resembles coarse crumbs. Stir in ¾ cup water; stir in additional water to make a stiff dough. Turn dough onto lightly floured board. Beat dough with wooden spoon or mallet 5 minutes, turning and folding dough constantly. Roll or pat dough to ¼-inch thickness. Cut with 2-inch biscuit cutter.

Place biscuits on ungreased cookie sheet; prick tops with fork. Bake 18 to 20 minutes or until golden brown.

24 biscuits.

A plate of Sunday dinner with Fried Oysters with Dipping Sauce, Beaten Biscuits, Snap Bean Salad and Ginger-Wine Baked Ham.

Snap Bean Salad

───────◆───────

Herb Dressing (below)

½ *pound fresh green beans, cut into 1-inch pieces*

1 *head Boston lettuce, torn into pieces (about 3 cups)*

¼ *cup chopped fresh savory or parsley*

Prepare Herb Dressing. Cook green beans in boiling water 4 to 5 minutes until crisp-tender; drain and cool. Mix lettuce and savory with green beans; drizzle with Herb Dressing.

Herb Dressing

¼ *cup vegetable oil*

2 *tablespoons tarragon vinegar*

1 *tablespoon chopped fresh or 1 teaspoon dried thyme leaves*

1 *tablespoon chopped fresh or 1 teaspoon dried savory leaves*

½ *teaspoon Dijon mustard*

¼ *teaspoon pepper*

Whisk all ingredients in small bowl until well blended.

Serving of Indian Pudding with Berries.

Ginger-Wine Baked Ham

---◆---

1 to 1½ pounds fully cooked boneless smoked ham

2 cups dry white wine or apple juice

¼ cup bourbon or apple juice

1 teaspoon ground ginger

Heat oven to 350°. Place ham on large piece of aluminum foil in square baking dish, 8 × 8 × 2 inches. Pour wine and bourbon over ham; sprinkle with ginger. Seal foil tightly around ham. Bake 30 minutes or until ham is hot.

Indian Pudding with Berries

---◆---

½ cup sugar

1 teaspoon ground cinnamon

½ teaspoon ground ginger

¼ teaspoon salt

¼ teaspoon ground nutmeg

4 cups milk

½ cup yellow cornmeal

½ cup molasses

2 tablespoons margarine or butter

2 eggs, beaten

1 cup fresh blueberries

Heat oven to 350°. Mix sugar, cinnamon, ginger, salt and nutmeg until well blended; reserve.

Heat milk to scalding in large saucepan; stir in cornmeal. Cook over low heat, stirring constantly, about 20 minutes or until very thick. Remove from heat; stir in sugar mixture and remaining ingredients except berries.

Pour into greased 2-quart casserole. Place casserole in rectangular pan, 13 × 9 × 2 inches, on oven rack. Pour very hot water into pan to depth of 1 inch. Bake 55 to 60 minutes or until knife inserted in center comes out clean. Serve warm with berries. Pour cream over pudding or serve with whipped cream if desired.

Soup and Salad Luncheon

Kiwifruit Salad*

Fresh Salmon Chowder*

Orange-Rye Muffins*

Rhubarb Meringue Pie*

Grapefruit Juice and Sparkling Water

Serves 8

*L*uncheons used to have a "ladies only" reputation, but today they are much more universal. Luncheons are an attractive entertaining idea as people like to eat less at lunch, so you can concentrate on just a few dishes, and everyone will feel satisfied and well fed. A luncheon on a Saturday can be an easy get-together for friends between errands and evening plans, an informal opportunity to welcome a new neighbor or to say "thank you" to the couple who took care of your cat when you went on vacation. You can arrange the party any way you want when lunch is on you.

THE FINISHING TOUCH

◆ Fill a soup tureen with an arrangement of pink and red tulips, and place a favorite piece of folk art on the table to complete the centerpiece. A wooden cow doorstop, horse weathervane or a wooden Noah's ark are examples of the sorts of charming objects you might consider. You can be creative in looking through your house—try pieces on the table before the party until you get just the right look.

◆ Use a plaid or striped cloth with colored napkins. A red plaid cloth will give a masculine look, and yet work nicely with the flowers. Tie napkins with red ribbons to match the tablecloth and flowers.

◆ Red, dark green or blue plates look nice on this table. You can mix colors of soup and salad plates, as long as they coordinate with each other.

◆ Wrap small jars of jams, teas or pasta in baskets or a wooden bird feeder to give as a gift to a new neighbor or to thank a friend.

◆ Consider serving coffee and tea in the living room, or if the day is nice, outside on the porch. On the porch you can enjoy lunch and a beautiful spring day.

Informal presentation of Soup and Salad Luncheon showing whimsical folk art centerpiece.

Kiwifruit Salad

———————✦———————

Champagne Vinegar Dressing (right)

1 small bunch romaine lettuce, torn into bite-size pieces (about 10 cups)

1 avocado, peeled, pitted and sliced

3 kiwifruit, peeled and sliced

Prepare Champagne Vinegar Dressing. Place lettuce in salad bowl; top with avocado and kiwifruit. Drizzle with dressing.

Champagne Vinegar Dressing

½ cup champagne vinegar

¼ cup vegetable oil

1 tablespoon sugar

1 tablespoon Dijon mustard

Shake all ingredients in tightly covered jar until well blended.

Fresh Salmon Chowder

———✦———

Fresh salmon, lovely all year, is particularly delicious in the spring. Dill weed complements its fresh flavor.

Fresh Salmon Chowder

3 slices bacon, chopped

2 medium leeks, thinly sliced

1 clove garlic, crushed

⅓ cup chopped fresh or 2 tablespoons dried dill weed

¾ teaspoon salt

½ teaspoon white pepper

2 cups fish stock or clam juice

1½ pounds small red potatoes, cut into 1-inch pieces

1 pound fresh or frozen salmon fillet, skinned and cut into 1-inch pieces

4 cups half-and-half

1 cup fresh or frozen whole kernel corn

Cook bacon in large saucepan over medium heat until crisp. Drain fat, reserving 1 tablespoon. Cook leeks and garlic in fat about 5 minutes until leeks are soft. Stir in dill weed, salt, white pepper, fish stock and potatoes.

Cook uncovered over low heat 15 to 20 minutes until potatoes are tender, but not soft. Add remaining ingredients and cook 10 to 15 minutes until salmon is done.

Orange-Rye Muffins

———✦———

1¼ cups all-purpose flour

¾ cup rye flour

2 tablespoons sugar

3 teaspoons baking powder

¼ teaspoon salt

½ cup orange juice

½ cup vegetable oil

1 tablespoon grated orange peel

2 eggs

1 tablespoon sugar

Heat oven to 400°. Grease 12 medium muffin cups, 2½ × 1¼ inches, or line with paper baking cups. Mix flours, 2 tablespoons sugar, baking powder and salt in large bowl. Stir in remaining ingredients except 1 tablespoon sugar, just until moistened. Fill muffin cups two-thirds full. Sprinkle batter with 1 tablespoon sugar. Bake 12 to 18 minutes until muffins are golden brown. Remove from pan; cool. *12 muffins.*

Rhubarb Meringue Pie

Rhubarb Meringue Pie

———————— ✦ ————————

Tart rhubarb is a wonderful contrast to the pie's sweet meringue topping.

> *9-inch baked pie shell (right)*
> *2 eggs*
> *1 cup sugar*
> *⅓ cup all-purpose flour*
> *4 cups cut-up rhubarb*
> *2 tablespoons margarine or butter*
> *3 egg whites*
> *¼ teaspoon cream of tartar*
> *¼ cup sugar*

Prepare and bake pie shell. Heat oven to 375°. Beat together eggs and 1 cup sugar in large bowl until thick. Stir in flour and rhubarb; pour into baked pastry shell. Dot with margarine. Bake 35 to 45 minutes until filling is bubbly and rhubarb is tender. Cool pie on wire rack.

Heat oven to 400°. Beat egg whites and cream of tartar in large bowl until foamy. Beat in ¼ cup sugar, 1 tablespoon at a time; continue to beat until stiff and glossy. Spread meringue over filling to edge of crust. Bake 6 to 8 minutes until delicate brown. Cool pie away from draft.

Baked Pie Shell

> *1 cup all-purpose flour*
> *½ teaspoon salt*
> *6 tablespoons shortening, cut into pieces*
> *2 to 3 tablespoons iced water*

Heat oven to 475°. Place flour and salt in food processor. Add shortening; cover and process 10 seconds until mixture resembles coarse meal. With machine running, add iced water until pastry holds together.

Gather pastry into a ball on lightly floured surface. Roll pastry 2 inches larger than 9-inch pie plate. Ease pastry into plate; prick bottom and side with fork. Bake 8 to 10 minutes until light golden brown.

CONVENTIONAL METHOD:

Cut shortening into flour and salt with pastry blender until mixture resembles coarse meal. Sprinkle in water, 1 tablespoon at a time, tossing with fork until almost all flour is moistened and pastry cleans side of bowl.

Bird feeder packed with gifts (see page 36).

Summer

Dinner Under the Stars

Summer Sunsets*

Pasta with Lemon and Basil*

Grilled Tuna with Salsa*

Grilled Summer Squash*

Pepper-Cheese Twists*

Peach Schaum Torte with Caramel Sauce*

Coffee and Tea

Serves 6

Stargazing is an excellent summer activity, and this menu takes advantage of a fine night to give guests an elegant dinner as well as a view of the heavens. The night sky has cast a spell on people for centuries with twinkling stars, changing constellations and the beauty of the moon. When your guests follow the star charts that have been set at their places, the stars will point the way to a heavenly meal and a memorable evening.

THE FINISHING TOUCH

◆ Use an elegant crystal or silver vase for the centerpiece, and fill with flowers such as full-blown roses, lilies, trailing clematises or cleomes to create an impressive display. You can also use a silver ice bucket with a removable lid as an elegant vase.

◆ Set out silver or crystal candlesticks, whichever best matches your vase.

◆ Drape the table with a large sheet in a pretty floral pattern that complements your centerpiece. (Be sure to use a flat sheet, not a contour sheet.) Tie each corner with ribbon in an appropriate color, and fasten flowers that coordinate with the centerpiece to each corner of the table. (See photo at right.)

Preceding pages: *Dinner Under the Stars*

- Use either white or solid-color cloth napkins, and tie a small flower to each napkin with ribbon. Set out a tablecloth patterned with cabbage roses, roses at each corner of the table and roses tied to each napkin for a lovely summer motif.
- This is the time to use your best dishes, preferably silver and white or other unpatterned dishes. Use clear stemware and your nicest flatware.
- Place a star chart that shows the sky for your area at each place. Make a cover of construction paper for each chart, put on some glue, then sprinkle the cover with glitter for a star effect.
- Put a kaleidoscope tied with ribbon at each place. If you are eating inside, guests can use them to make their own stars. Outside, they will come in handy if the sky clouds over.
- Play classical music, such as Holst's *The Planets*.
- If dinner is served in an apartment, take guests up to the roof for tea and coffee, and enjoy the night sky. If you eat in the house, go out to the yard after dinner.

Tablecloth tied at the corner with summer flowers (left). Place setting showing star chart and kaleidoscope (below).

Pasta with Lemon and Basil

Summer Sunsets

———◆———

Mix all ingredients, except sparkling water, before the party and refrigerate. Add sparkling water just before serving.

>   *3 cups cranberry apricot juice*
>   *1 bottle (25 ounces) dry white wine or white grape juice*
>   *1 bottle (16 ounces) sparkling water*
>   *1 medium apricot, sliced*

Mix all ingredients in 2- to 2½-quart pitcher. Serve over ice with slice of apricot.

>   *6 servings.*

Pasta with Lemon and Basil

———◆———

>   *6 ounces angel hair pasta*
>   *¼ cup chopped fresh basil leaves*
>   *¼ cup lemon juice*
>   *1 tablespoon grated lemon peel*
>   *3 tablespoons olive oil*
>   *½ teaspoon black pepper*
>   *Grated Parmesan cheese*

Cook pasta in boiling water 3 to 5 minutes or just until tender; drain. Toss with remaining ingredients except cheese. Serve with cheese.

Grilled Tuna
with Salsa

———————◆———————

To seed tomatoes, cut in half crosswise and squeeze gently—the seeds will be released easily.

¾ cup finely chopped fresh parsley

¼ cup finely chopped onion

⅓ cup lemon juice

2 tablespoons vegetable oil

¼ teaspoon salt

2 medium tomatoes, seeded and chopped

1 clove garlic, crushed

1 can (4¼ ounces) chopped black olives, drained

6 tuna or shark steaks (about 5 ounces each)

Combine all ingredients except tuna in glass bowl. Cover tightly and refrigerate salsa 2 to 4 hours to blend flavors.

Place tuna on oiled grill over medium-hot coals. Cook 3 minutes; turn steaks and cook 4 to 5 minutes or until tuna turns opaque in center. Remove from grill; keep warm. Serve with salsa.

TO BROIL:

Set oven control to broil. Arrange steaks on oiled rack in broiler pan. Broil with steaks about 4 inches from heat 10 to 15 minutes, turning after 6 minutes, until fish flakes easily with fork.

Grilled Tuna with Salsa

Grilled Summer Squash

———◆———

2 medium zucchini

2 medium yellow squash

24 small patty pan squash or cherry tomatoes

¼ cup olive oil

Dill Butter (below)

Cut zucchini and yellow squash into 1-inch pieces. Thread squash, zucchini and tomatoes onto 10-inch metal skewers; brush with olive oil. Grill 5 to 6 inches from medium coals about 8 minutes, turning several times, until squash is tender. Serve with Dill Butter.

Dill Butter

½ cup butter or margarine

3 tablespoons chopped fresh or 1 tablespoon dried dill weed

Mix butter and dill weed until well blended.

Pepper-Cheese Twists

———◆———

These are easy to make ahead; just cover tightly until ready to serve.

½ package (17¼ ounces) frozen puff pastry dough, thawed

1 egg, beaten

1 cup shredded Cheddar cheese

2 teaspoons black pepper

Heat oven to 425°. Roll sheet of dough into 18 × 12-inch rectangle; brush with beaten egg. Sprinkle cheese over half of rectangle; fold remaining half over cheese and press edges to seal. Brush dough with egg; sprinkle with pepper. Cut pastry lengthwise into ½-inch strips. Twist strips and place on cookie sheet. Bake 10 to 12 minutes or until light golden brown.

18 twists.

Pepper-Cheese Twists and a Summer Sunset.

Peach Schaum Torte with Caramel Sauce

Peach Schaum Torte with Caramel Sauce

The meringue base for this impressive torte can be baked the day before the party. Top with ice cream, peaches and caramel sauce just before serving. Make caramel sauce ahead and refrigerate. Reheat sauce over low heat about 8 minutes, stirring occasionally. Serve dessert with hot coffee and tea and have bowls of whipped cream, grated lemon and orange peel for guests to add to beverages.

> 8 egg whites
> 1 tablespoon vinegar
> ½ teaspoon cream of tartar
> 2½ cups sugar
> Vanilla ice cream
> 6 ripe peaches, sliced
> Caramel Sauce (right)

Heat oven to 275°. Make a 4-inch band of aluminum foil 2 inches longer than circumference of springform pan, 9 × 3 inches. Extend pan by securing band around outside edge. Beat egg whites with vinegar and cream of tartar in large bowl until foamy. Gradually beat in sugar; continue beating until stiff and glossy. Do not underbeat. Spoon into springform pan.

Bake meringue 1½ hours. Turn oven off; leave meringue in oven with door closed 1 hour. Finish cooling at room temperature. Prepare Caramel Sauce. Serve meringue topped with vanilla ice cream, peaches and Caramel Sauce.

Caramel Sauce

> 1 cup packed brown sugar
> ½ cup half-and-half
> ¼ cup light corn syrup
> 1 tablespoon margarine or butter

Heat all ingredients in small saucepan over medium heat, stirring constantly; reduce heat to low. Simmer uncovered 5 minutes. Serve warm.

Weekend Brunch

Vegetable-Sausage Strata*

Melon Salad*

Brown Sugar Muffins*

Peach-Plum Kuchen*

Juice

Coffee and Tea

Serves 8

Hurrah *for the weekend! After the stress and strain of the week, Sunday brunch is a friendly and informal way to relax with family, friends or a combination of family and friends. People like to linger over brunch, and in summer this inclination seems stronger. The lure of a long summer afternoon is even more appealing when you serve this delicious brunch. Be sure to have beverages available throughout the afternoon, and provide ice for people who prefer iced coffee and tea in hot weather. You may want to save the Peach-Plum Kuchen to serve later in the afternoon when people are ready for "a little something."*

THE FINISHING TOUCH

◆ For a centerpiece, heap a selection of summer fruits, such as peaches, apricots, cherries, grapes and berries, on a footed stand. Let people help themselves during brunch and throughout the afternoon.

◆ Use a simple cloth—pale yellow or peach are good summer choices—and set out floral cloth napkins that echo the colors of the fruit.

◆ Bring out your Fiesta ware or mix and match colorful pieces from different sets of china.

✦ Buy at least two copies of your favorite Sunday paper or papers, and pass the sections around for everyone to enjoy.

✦ Have a crossword puzzle contest; divide guests into two teams and let each team wrestle with the crossword puzzle. Whichever team finishes first gets dibs on the sections of the paper they want—including the comics!

✦ Move away from the table when brunch is over, and relax in the living room, on the porch or on the lawn. Show guests where the beverages are, and let them help themselves throughout the afternoon.

Vegetable-Sausage Strata

———✦———

The strata is best assembled the day before—but don't bake it then. Cover and refrigerate, then bake in the morning and serve hot.

1 medium onion, chopped

1 pound pork sausage

1 loaf French bread (about 10 inches), cut into ½-inch slices

2 medium tomatoes, sliced

2 medium zucchini, sliced

½ cup ricotta cheese

¼ cup chopped fresh or 2 tablespoons dried basil leaves

6 eggs

2 cups milk

Cook onion and sausage over medium heat in 10-inch skillet 15 minutes, stirring frequently, until sausage is done; drain well. Line bottom of 2-quart round or oval baking dish with bread slices. Top bread with sausage mixture. Arrange tomato and zucchini slices over sausage mixture. Spoon cheese over vegetables; sprinkle with basil. Beat eggs in medium bowl; stir in milk. Pour over entire mixture. Cover and refrigerate at least 2 hours or overnight.

Heat oven to 350°. Bake strata uncovered 45 to 55 minutes until puffed and set in center. Serve immediately.

Melon Salad

———✦———

Make this pretty fruit salad ahead of time. The flavors intensify during refrigeration.

½ medium cantaloupe

½ medium honeydew

½ medium watermelon

½ cup orange juice

1 tablespoon grated orange peel

Cut melons into cubes or scoop into balls; toss with orange juice and orange peel in large bowl. Cover and refrigerate at least 1 hour.

Brown Sugar Muffins

———♦———

1 cup quick-cooking oats

½ cup milk

¾ cup packed brown sugar

¼ cup margarine or butter, melted

1 egg

1 cup all-purpose flour

½ cup chopped walnuts

2 teaspoons baking powder

Heat oven to 400°. Grease 12 medium muffin cups, 2½ × 1¼ inches. Mix oats, milk and brown sugar in large bowl; let stand 5 minutes. Add margarine and egg; blend well. Stir in remaining ingredients just until moistened. Fill muffin cups two-thirds full. Bake 15 to 20 minutes or until wooden pick inserted in center comes out clean.

12 muffins.

Peach-Plum Kuchen

———♦———

½ cup margarine or butter, softened

¼ cup packed brown sugar

¼ teaspoon almond extract

1 egg

1 cup all-purpose flour

½ teaspoon baking powder

¼ teaspoon salt

2 peaches, cut into thin slices

3 plums, cut into thin slices

¼ cup peach jam, melted

Heat oven to 350°. Grease tart pan, 9 × 1 inch. Beat together margarine and brown sugar in large bowl; stir in almond extract and egg. Add flour, baking powder and salt; stir until well blended. Press dough onto bottom and side of tart pan. Arrange peaches and plums over dough. Bake 30 to 35 minutes until edges are golden brown. Cool 10 minutes; remove side of pan. Brush top of kuchen with peach jam.

Fourth of July Picnic

Crab Claws*

Fireworks Salad*

Flank Steak in Garlic Pitas*

Melon Basket with Berries*

Raspberry Brownie Thins*

Strawberry Ice Cream*

Fresh Fruit Juices

Serves 10

*T*he founders of our country probably didn't foresee that Independence Day would be celebrated with barbecues and picnics, but that has become our tradition. No doubt the fact it's a holiday that must be celebrated on a given day—no time shifting for the Fourth of July!—gives people a great excuse to enjoy a summer day, regardless of when it falls in the week. Independence Day is the time to be unabashedly patriotic— use a red, white and blue motif, and celebrate.

THE FINISHING TOUCH

◆ Decorate your yard in red, white and blue. Balloons and colored pinwheels work nicely. If you don't have a yard, make this an indoor picnic, and decorate your dining room or dining area. A folk art figure of Uncle Sam adds a lively and nostalgic touch. So does folk art that incorporates the American flag.

✦ Carry on the red, white and blue theme in your centerpiece by filling a large blue bowl with ripe strawberries, and dusting with powdered sugar—or fill a white three-tiered basket with strawberries. Another lovely centerpiece is a white basket filled with red flowers such as roses, petunias and zinnias. Surround this with blue votive candles.

✦ Let your dishes echo the motif as much as possible, short of buying all new dishes. Use combinations of red, white and blue—perhaps borrow plates or serving pieces in appropriate colors and patterns from friends who are coming to the picnic. Use red, white and blue glasses.

✦ Tie red napkins with blue and white ribbons, or use metallic ribbons with stars.

✦ Cover the picnic table—or your table inside—with a blue cloth to continue the red, white and blue theme. You may want to use a quilt as a tablecloth. Be sure it's a washable quilt and not a delicate antique, as food will no doubt be spilled on it.

✦ Set up a croquet game, start a friendly softball game or organize sack races.

✦ Ask guests to help churn the ice cream, and set the ice-cream freezer in the shade when ready to serve.

✦ Have a contest to see who can quote the most of the Declaration of Independence, the document signed on July 4, 1776. Give everyone the first few words, "When in the course of human events," and let your guests take it from there. Award the winner a box of tea (in honor of the Boston Tea Party) tagged with the colonial rallying cry, "No taxation without representation!"

✦ Choose music to suit the day, and your taste—anything from John Philip Sousa marches to "It's a Grand Old Flag" to Bruce Springsteen's "Born in the USA."

Strawberries, flags, metallic ribbon with stars and an Uncle Sam whirligig create a patriotic centerpiece.

Crab Claws

If you can't find fresh crab claws, substitute frozen crab claws. If you'd like, substitute less expensive imitation crab sticks for the crab claws.

1 pound cooked crab claws

1 cup sour cream

¼ cup prepared horseradish

2 tablespoons finely chopped parsley

1 teaspoon Worcestershire sauce

Rinse crab claws in cold water to remove loose pieces of shell. Cover and refrigerate. Mix remaining ingredients in medium bowl until well blended. Serve sauce with crab claws.

Fireworks Salad

◆

1 package (10 ounces) Chinese noodles,
   cooked and drained

1 medium yellow bell pepper, thinly sliced

1 medium red bell pepper, thinly sliced

½ pound sugar snap peas, cooked

1 cup shredded green cabbage

6 green onions, chopped (about ⅓ cup)

1 can (8 ounces) water chestnuts, drained
   and cut into fourths

3 tablespoons soy sauce

3 tablespoons dry sherry or chicken broth

2 tablespoons sesame oil

1 teaspoon sugar

½ to 1 teaspoon red pepper sauce

Mix noodles, bell peppers, peas, cabbage, onions and water chestnuts in large bowl. Whisk together remaining ingredients; pour over vegetable mixture and toss to coat. Cover and refrigerate at least 1 hour to blend flavors.

Flank Steak in Garlic Pitas

◆

2 flank steaks (2 pounds each)

¼ cup honey

2 tablespoons soy sauce

1 tablespoon grated fresh gingerroot

1 can (12 ounces) beer or 1½ cups beef
   broth

Garlic Pitas (right)

Trim fat from steaks. Cut both sides of beef into diamond pattern ⅛ inch deep. Place in shallow glass dish. Mix remaining ingredients except Garlic Pitas; pour over beef. Cover and refrigerate at least 4 hours, turning occasionally.

Remove beef from marinade; reserve marinade. Prepare Garlic Pitas. Grill steaks 6 inches from medium coals about 12 minutes, turning after 6 minutes, and brushing frequently with marinade. Cut diagonally into thin slices; serve on Garlic Pitas.

TO BROIL:

Set oven control to broil. Broil beef with top 2 to 3 inches from heat about 5 minutes or until brown. Turn beef; brush with marinade. Broil 5 minutes longer.

Garlic Pitas

½ cup margarine or butter, softened

2 cloves garlic, crushed

10 pita breads (6 inches in diameter)

Mix margarine and garlic in small bowl. Spread pita bread with margarine mixture. Wrap in foil and heat on grill 5 minutes until margarine melts.

OVEN PITAS:

Heat oven to 350°. Place wrapped pita breads in oven; bake 5 to 10 minutes until margarine melts.

Following pages: *Fourth of July Picnic*

An easy-to-make melon basket (see recipe below) with red, white and blue tableware.

Melon Basket
with Berries

———◆———

This festive fruit basket displays patriotic fruit!

1 large honeydew or cantaloupe

1 cup blueberries, raspberries or blackberries

5 slices watermelon

5 slices cantaloupe

Draw a 1-inch-wide "handle" across honeydew with a pencil. Cut top 2 inches off honeydew, leaving "handle" uncut. Scoop out seeds. Cut top of melon with sharp knife to form scalloped edge. Scoop inside flesh of honeydew into balls; fill honeydew with melon balls and berries. Surround melon basket with watermelon and cantaloupe slices.

Raspberry Brownie Thins

———◆———

½ cup margarine or butter

½ cup unsweetened cocoa

1 cup granulated sugar

½ cup all-purpose flour

¼ cup seedless raspberry jam

1 teaspoon vanilla

2 eggs, beaten

Powdered sugar

Heat oven to 350°. Grease bottom of rectangular pan, 13 × 9 × 2 inches. Melt margarine and stir in cocoa until well blended; stir in granulated sugar. Mix cocoa mixture and remaining ingredients except powdered sugar until batter is smooth. Spread evenly into pan. Bake 10 to 12 minutes until batter begins to pull away from side of pan. Cool on rack; cut into squares. Sprinkle with powdered sugar.

About 36 brownies.

Strawberry Ice Cream

———————◆———————

1 quart fresh strawberries, washed and hulled

½ cup sugar

2 cups whipping (heavy) cream

1 cup milk

¼ cup sugar

½ teaspoon vanilla

2 eggs

Mix strawberries and ½ cup sugar in bowl; let stand about 1 hour, stirring occasionally. Mash strawberries.

Whisk together remaining ingredients. Cook in medium saucepan over low heat, stirring constantly, about 8 minutes until mixture thickens. Stir in strawberry mixture. Chill mixture about 2 hours. Pour into ice-cream freezer; freeze according to manufacturer's directions.

1 quart.

Strawberry Ice Cream, made in the shade.

Grilled Summer Supper

Steak with Peppercorns*

Grilled Zucchini with Basil*

Lemony Potato Salad*

Mint Iced Tea*

Chocolate-Nectarine Shortcake*

Serves 6

With this easy, informal menu you can take the advice of the old song and "roll out the lazy, hazy, crazy days of summer." Make it a family evening or invite friends over for this relaxed supper. You can take it easy too, knowing that most of the meal can be prepared ahead; all you'll need to do to get dinner on the table is grill the steaks. If you don't have a yard, or if the weather's just too hot and sticky for comfort, use your broiler instead of the grill and have an indoor supper. Wherever you eat, get comfortable, relax and enjoy some summer fun.

THE FINISHING TOUCH

◆ Pick common wildflowers to fill a crock with a casual bouquet. Look for butterfly weed, boneset, Queen Anne's lace, black-eyed Susan, yarrow, ironweed, sunflower, meadow rue or other local flowers. Keep in mind this friendly rule for picking wild-flowers: Don't pick more than one flower out of a stand of five.

◆ Cover your picnic table with a length of striped ticking—blue and white is a cooling color combination. Fasten the ticking with thumbtacks on the underside of the table for a quick slipcover look.

◆ Place silverware, dishes and napkins in baskets, and carry outside to the table, then let everyone help themselves. If you are eating inside, use the baskets to carry these items to your "picnic" spot—the sun room, an enclosed porch, or a blanket on the dining room floor—wherever you are most comfortable.

✦ If you are outside, "borrow" some fireflies to make a lantern. Catch fireflies in a glass jar with air holes in the lid, and let them light your table for a bit. Be sure to open the jar and return the fireflies to nature before the evening ends.

✦ When it's time for dessert, invite everyone into the kitchen to create their own Chocolate-Nectarine Shortcake. Set out the shortcakes, sliced fruit and sauce, then let your guests serve themselves.

Steak with Peppercorns

———◆———

3 tablespoons cracked black peppercorns

6 boneless sirloin steaks (about ¾ inch thick)

1 tablespoon margarine or butter

¼ cup finely chopped shallots

¼ cup brandy or beef broth

½ cup beef broth

½ cup sour cream

Press peppercorns into both sides of steaks. Grill steaks 5 to 6 inches from medium coals 3 to 5 minutes per side or until desired doneness.

Melt margarine in medium saucepan over medium heat; add shallots. Cook about 2 minutes until shallots are tender. Stir in brandy and broth; cook over medium-high heat about 5 minutes or until mixture is slightly reduced. Stir in sour cream. Serve with steaks.

TO BROIL:

Set oven control to broil. Place steaks on rack in broiler pan; place pan 2 to 3 inches from heat. Broil 10 minutes; turn steaks. Broil 8 to 10 minutes or until desired doneness.

Grilled Zucchini with Basil

———◆———

¼ cup olive oil

2 tablespoons chopped fresh or 2 teaspoons dried basil leaves

¼ teaspoon salt

¼ teaspoon pepper

6 medium zucchini, cut in half lengthwise

Mix all ingredients except zucchini. Place zucchini cut side up on grill 5 to 6 inches from medium coals; brush with oil mixture. Grill about 3 to 5 minutes until slightly soft. Turn zucchini over; brush with oil mixture and grill 2 minutes until tender.

TO BROIL:

Set oven control to broil. Arrange zucchini on rack in broiler pan; brush with oil mixture. Broil with zucchini 4 inches from heat 3 to 5 minutes. Turn over; brush with oil mixture and broil about 2 minutes until tender.

Lemony Potato Salad

———————◆———————

Make this refreshing salad in the morning for a no-fuss supper. No need to cool the potatoes; just add them directly to the salad.

½ cup chopped onion

1 tablespoon grated lemon peel

¼ cup lemon juice

1 tablespoon vegetable oil

1 teaspoon salt

2 pounds new potatoes, cooked, peeled and diced

1 cup chopped celery

½ cup mayonnaise

1 medium cucumber, peeled, seeded and chopped

1 yellow bell pepper, chopped

Mix onion, lemon peel, lemon juice, oil and salt in large bowl. Stir in potatoes; toss to coat. Cover and refrigerate at least 1 hour. Stir in remaining ingredients. Cover and refrigerate until ready to serve.

Mint Iced Tea

———————◆———————

8 cups cold water

1 cup packed fresh mint leaves

6 tea bags

Combine all ingredients in 2-quart pitcher. Stir to bruise mint leaves. Refrigerate overnight. Remove tea bags and mint leaves. Serve in tall glasses with ice. Serve with sugar if desired.

2 quarts.

Chocolate-Nectarine Shortcake

———————◆———————

Prepare Nectarine-Strawberry Sauce when you have a few minutes, and keep in the refrigerator until ready to serve.

1½ cups all-purpose flour

⅓ cup unsweetened cocoa

⅓ cup sugar

2 teaspoons baking powder

¾ teaspoon baking soda

6 tablespoons margarine or butter

1 cup milk

6 medium nectarines, pitted and sliced

Nectarine-Strawberry Sauce (below)

Heat oven to 425°. Grease cookie sheet. Blend flour, cocoa, sugar, baking powder and baking soda in large bowl; cut in margarine with pastry blender until mixture resembles coarse crumbs. Stir in milk until well blended.

Divide dough into 6 parts; drop dough onto cookie sheet. Bake 10 to 12 minutes or until done. Let cool. Prepare Nectarine-Strawberry Sauce. Split each shortcake horizontally in half. Spoon about ½ cup sliced nectarines on each of 6 halves. Top with remaining half shortcake. Spoon 2 tablespoons sauce over each shortcake.

Nectarine-Strawberry Sauce

½ pint strawberries

2 tablespoons sugar

1 tablespoon lemon juice

2 medium nectarines, pitted and chopped

Place all ingredients in blender. Cover and blend until smooth.

Cool Lunch
for a Hot Day

Summer Fruit Coolers*

Cold Raspberry Soup*

Gazpacho Pasta Salad*

Marinated Shrimp*

Macadamia-Lemon Bars*

Serves 6

If you can't stand the heat, don't heat up the kitchen! With this refreshing menu you can keep cool and prepare a satisfying, substantial lunch at the same time. Bake the Macadamia Lemon Bars the night before, and broil the shrimp in the cool of the morning, allowing them time to chill before lunch. While preparing the rest of the meal, there's no need to turn on the oven and swelter in the kitchen. You'll enjoy the cool charm of this pleasant lunch, which is never too hot to handle.

THE FINISHING TOUCH

◆ Noon is the hottest time of the day, so serve lunch under a large umbrella or in the shade of a tree. Consider moving lunch indoors if the mercury soars or humidity makes the outdoors too oppressive.

◆ Serve on clear or lightly colored glass plates for a cool look. Set out glass goblets in complementary colors.

◆ Keep an eye out for roadside produce stands and urban farmer's markets. Take advantage of their summer bounty and buy the raspberries, tomatoes, peppers, cucumbers and green onions for this menu.

◆ This is a great menu for a vacation house at the beach, lake, mountains or other spot. Assign a different dish to each person, and serve the meal when people are hungry. This is definitely a lunch that can be made at different times by different people—perfect for a group with individual schedules.

◆ Make fans for guests out of construction paper. Fold paper like an accordion, then cut designs in the edges of the paper as you would for snowflakes. Punch a hole toward bottom of fan and secure with ribbon or raffia.

◆ Tie a large bunch of ivy with pale blue or green ribbon and attach it to the front door as a cool greeting.

Summer Fruit Coolers

◆

2 tablespoons sugar

1 cup sparkling water

½ cup orange juice

1 bottle (25 ounces) dry white wine or white grape juice

½ cup halved green grapes

1 medium orange, cut into halves and thinly sliced

1 kiwifruit, peeled and sliced

Mix sugar, sparkling water, orange juice and wine in large pitcher. Stir in fruit. Chill for 1 hour. Serve coolers over ice.

Cold Raspberry Soup

◆

Because of their rich flavor, cold fruit soups are Scandinavian favorites, and no doubt this will be a hit with you as well.

4 cups fresh raspberries

½ cup sugar

¼ cup dry red wine or cranberry juice

1 cup sour cream

Place raspberries, sugar and wine in blender. Cover and blend until smooth. Stir in sour cream. Cover and refrigerate 1 to 2 hours until cold. Serve with dollops of sour cream and raspberries if desired.

Left: *Cold Raspberry Soup.* Opposite: *Cool Lunch for a Hot Day, served invitingly under a shady umbrella.*

Gazpacho Pasta Salad

—————◆—————

1 pound rotini pasta, cooked and drained

½ cup finely chopped fresh cilantro leaves

8 green onions, chopped (about ½ cup)

2 large tomatoes, seeded and chopped (about 2 cups)

1 small red bell pepper, chopped (about ½ cup)

1 small yellow bell pepper, chopped (about ½ cup)

1 large cucumber, peeled and chopped (about 1½ cups)

1 green Anaheim chili, seeded and chopped (about ¼ cup)

Lime Vinaigrette (below)

Combine all ingredients in large bowl until well blended. Prepare and pour Lime Vinaigrette over salad; toss to coat.

Lime Vinaigrette

½ cup olive oil

½ cup lime juice

½ teaspoon salt

¼ teaspoon pepper

2 cloves garlic, crushed

1 bottle (10 ounces) tomato juice

Mix all ingredients.

Marinated Shrimp

—————◆—————

1½ pounds large raw shrimp, shelled and deveined

1 tablespoon soy sauce

1 tablespoon lemon juice

1 teaspoon vegetable oil

1 teaspoon finely chopped fresh gingerroot

Place shrimp in glass baking dish. Mix remaining ingredients; pour over shrimp. Cover and refrigerate at least 30 minutes.

Set oven control to broil. Drain shrimp; arrange on rack in broiler pan. Broil 4 inches from heat 5 to 8 minutes, turning once, until shrimp turn pink. Refrigerate shrimp at least 30 minutes until cold.

Summer Fruit Cooler and Marinated Shrimp with homemade fans (see page 62).

Macadamia-Lemon Bars

———◆———

1 cup all-purpose flour

½ cup margarine or butter

¼ cup powdered sugar

¼ cup chopped macadamia nuts

2 eggs

1 cup granulated sugar

2 tablespoons lemon juice

2 teaspoons grated lemon peel

½ teaspoon baking powder

¼ teaspoon salt

2 tablespoons chopped macadamia nuts

Colorful fragrant flowers are always a welcome addition to a summer lunch.

Heat oven to 350°. Mix flour, margarine, powdered sugar and ¼ cup nuts in medium bowl. Press in ungreased square pan, 9 × 9 × 2 inches, building up ½-inch edges. Bake 20 minutes.

Beat remaining ingredients, except nuts, until light and fluffy. Pour over hot crust; sprinkle with nuts. Bake 20 to 25 minutes until no indentation remains when touched lightly in center; cool. Cut into bars.

25 bars.

Summer Wedding

Smoked Salmon Spread*

Pesto Pinwheels*

White Cheese Tomato Tart*

Lemon-Champagne Punch*

Chicken Strips with Mango Sauce*

Seafood-Rice Salad*

Beef Tenderloin on Herb Biscuits*

Fruit with Dip*

Wedding Cake

Champagne for Toasts

Coffee and Tea

Serves 20

*S*ummer *is particularly kind to brides—trees and flowers are in full bloom and the lovely weather turns backyards, parks and lawns into enticing spots for receptions. It's quite possible to host a wedding reception without becoming frazzled and frantic. With some easy organization you can enjoy the reception, share in the happiness of the newly married couple and not feel like a caterer! This is also why we recommend ordering the wedding cake from a bakery, though you can also order a plain cake and decorate it yourself with flowers that match the wedding flowers. Included in the recipes you'll find useful tips for how to prepare the food for the reception without overtaxing yourself.*

This menu is highly versatile and can be served as a luncheon, mid-afternoon meal or a dinner, whichever suits the bride and groom. Hosting a wedding reception is one of the loveliest presents you can give a couple. Whether it's for a member of your family or for a close friend, sharing your time and talent to create a memorable wedding reception not only is a present that will last forever but is one no couple ever has to return!

THE FINISHING TOUCH

✦ Confirm the colors the bride has chosen for the wedding, and use them in your decorations. We use a wedding built on a pretty daisy theme, the yellow and white of daisies echoed in the decorating ideas.

✦ Build a maypole for your centerpiece. Take a one-inch round dowel, forty-three inches long, and anchor it in a medium-size clay pot using plaster of paris. Wrap the pole in ribbons, alternating yellow and white. Place daisies securely on the top of the maypole, then attach four ribbons to the top as well. Each ribbon should be long enough to reach to a corner of your table. Fasten ribbons to the four corners of the table with a small bouquet of daisies and ivy. (If the wedding has a different color theme, use those colors in the ribbons, and match flowers accordingly.)

✦ Garland the table with ropes of daisies and ivy, anchored at the corners with bows of yellow and white ribbon. Tuck some fresh sweet marjoram, which signifies happiness, into the garlands. You can also add some sweet marjoram to the centerpiece.

✦ Cover the table with a white eyelet cloth over a solid yellow tablecloth so that the yellow peeps out subtly, looking almost like daisy petals. (If you are following a different color scheme, use a solid cloth in the dominant color, then cover with white eyelet.) Use large white linen napkins trimmed in white eyelet.

✦ It's not likely you'll have enough tableware for an event of this size, so investigate local rental shops, or try a local caterer to rent china, tableware and stemware. Look for the nicest pieces available in your price range. Rent white dishes, and stemware and silverware that harmonize as well as set an elegant tone.

✦ This wedding menu is perfect served outside. The reception can be held in a large yard, at a vacation home, at a local historic home or a park. Be sure to call and find out the restrictions, if any, for using a public space, and book the space well in advance of the wedding.

✦ As host, you are responsible for sending out invitations. Check with the bride and groom to see whether the invitations to the reception should be sent with their wedding invitations, or separately. The bride and groom will provide the guest list, as well as reserve veto power over the type of invitations you send out.

✦ Rent a tent for the occasion—a cheerful yellow and white tent is the right choice for this daisy wedding. A tent is absolutely essential if it rains, and it will also provide shade for an afternoon reception. At an evening reception, a tent allows the table to be lit easily, and gives a cozy feel to being outdoors.

✦ For a twilight or evening reception, set out yellow luminaria. Luminaria are lights made from votive candles—place yellow votive candles in paper bags filled with sand. Use yellow citronella candles to discourage bugs, and line the driveway, tent or dance floor with the luminaria.

✦ Also for an evening reception, place small "fairy" lights in the trees to twinkle through the evening. Use white lights, and avoid lights that blink, as they can be quite distracting.

✦ Live music for dancing is always the first choice, but sometimes budgets don't allow for it. If you don't have live music, consult the bride and groom a few weeks before the reception, and ask them for a list of their favorite types of music. Appoint a friend to play deejay, to bring tapes, CDs and records; to be responsible for setting up the sound system and to keep the music flowing throughout the reception. Be sure to ask what the couple would like as their first dance, and arrange at least one special

dance for members of the wedding party. It's also a nice idea to have a special song for a father/daughter dance as well as a mother/son dance.

✦ Instead of decorating the couple's car with "Just Married" signs, old shoes and tin cans, slip a "care package" basket in the front seat of the car. Fill a pretty basket with items to take on their honeymoon. For example, if they are going to the Caribbean, slip in some sunscreen, a good beach novel, matching sun visors, a bottle of flavored seltzer and so on.

✦ Keep a few bottles of champagne well chilled and bring them out to toast the couple when the cake is cut.

✦ Throw flower petals when the couple leaves the reception, instead of rice. Rice can sting when thrown, as well as get caught in hair and clothing. Throw daisy petals, or other flower petals that match the wedding flowers.

Smoked Salmon Spread

Prepare up to two days before the wedding. Refrigerate until ready to serve.

1 pound smoked salmon

1 cup sour cream

¼ cup chopped fresh or 2 tablespoons dried dill weed

4 green onions, chopped

40 slices cocktail thin rye or pumpernickel bread

Mix all ingredients except bread in medium bowl, breaking up salmon. Cover and refrigerate at least 2 hours to blend flavors. Spread on slices of bread. *2 cups.*

Pesto Pinwheels

Bake the pesto pinwheels the day before the wedding. They are delicious cold. Pesto is traditionally made with pine nuts for a distinctive Italian flavor; walnuts can successfully be substituted for a more pronounced basil flavor.

1 package (17¼ ounces) puff pastry dough, thawed

1 cup Pesto (right)

1 egg, beaten

Heat oven to 400°. Roll puff pastry into rectangle, 14 × 10 inches. Spread pastry with ½ cup pesto, leaving a ½-inch edge on long sides. Loosely roll dough from narrow end; brush seam with egg and pinch to seal. Slice into ½-inch slices. Place on ungreased cookie sheet. Bake 8 to 10 minutes or until golden brown. *40 pinwheels.*

Pesto

4 cups fresh basil leaves

½ cup pine nuts

¼ teaspoon salt

3 cloves garlic, peeled

½ cup olive oil

1 cup freshly grated Parmesan cheese

Place basil, nuts, salt and garlic in blender or food processor. Cover, blend or process until smooth. Slowly add oil with machine running to make a paste. Stir in cheese. *About 2 cups.*

White Cheese Tomato Tart

✦

You can make this tart the day before the wedding; refrigerate, then warm in the oven for about 15 minutes before serving. As this tart is very rich, small pieces make ample servings.

Tart Crust (right)

1 carton (15 ounces) ricotta cheese

½ pound Gruyère cheese, shredded

½ cup all-purpose flour

¼ cup margarine or butter

1 teaspoon salt

½ teaspoon white pepper

2 eggs

2 medium tomatoes, peeled and sliced

Prepare Tart Crust. Heat oven to 375°. Place all ingredients except tomato slices in food processor; cover and process 1 minute or until smooth. Spoon cheese mixture into tart crust. Arrange tomato slices over cheese mixture. Bake 20 to 25 minutes until top is light brown. Cool tart; remove side of pan. Cut into 1 × 1-inch pieces. Garnish pieces with fresh dill weed if desired. *About 100 pieces.*

Tart Crust

1 cup shortening

2⅔ cups all-purpose flour

1 teaspoon salt

7 to 8 tablespoons cold water

Heat oven to 475°. Cut shortening into flour and salt with pastry blender until mixture resembles coarse crumbs. Sprinkle in water, 1 tablespoon at a time, until pastry pulls away from side of bowl. Gather pastry into ball; flatten into round on lightly floured board. Roll pastry 2 inches larger than rectangular tart pan, 12 × 8 × 1 inch. Ease pastry into pan. Prick bottom and side of pastry with fork. Bake 8 to 10 minutes until light brown; cool.

Lemon-Champagne Punch

✦

2 quarts lemon sherbet

3 quarts champagne

1 cup brandy

Lemon slices

Strawberries

Mix all ingredients in large punch bowl. *About 40 servings.*

Chicken Strips with Mango Sauce

————◆————

The chicken strips can also be prepared ahead and refrigerated; serve either hot or cold with chilled sauce.

> ¼ cup olive oil
>
> 3 tablespoons soy sauce
>
> ½ cup dry sherry or apple juice
>
> 6 boneless skinless chicken breast halves (about ¾ pound each)
>
> Mango Sauce (below)

Mix oil, soy sauce and sherry in small bowl. Cut chicken into strips, 6 × 1 × ¼ inch. Pour marinade over chicken in glass pan. Cover and refrigerate at least 4 hours or overnight.

Set oven control to broil. Thread chicken onto 8-inch metal skewers. Cook 8 to 10 minutes, turning once, until done. Serve with Mango Sauce.

> 40 chicken strips.

Mango Sauce

> 2 mangoes or peaches, peeled, seeded and chopped
>
> 3 tablespoons honey
>
> ¼ cup lime juice

Place all ingredients in blender; cover and blend until smooth.

Seafood-Rice Salad

————◆————

Make this salad the day of the reception, and refrigerate until served. Garnish with flowers just before serving. Be sure to use unsprayed flowers.

> Lemon Vinaigette (below)
>
> 2 pounds scallops, cooked
>
> 1 pound medium shrimp, cooked and cleaned
>
> 4 cups cooked rice
>
> 3 cups broccoli flowerets, cooked
>
> 2 packages (6 ounces each) frozen crab-meat, thawed and drained

Prepare Lemon Vinaigrette. Mix all ingredients in large bowl except Lemon Vinaigrette. Toss salad with Lemon Vinaigrette. Sprinkle top with edible unsprayed flowers such as nasturtiums, violets or calendulas, if desired.

Lemon Vinaigrette

> ½ cup vegetable oil
>
> ½ cup lemon juice
>
> 2 tablespoons chopped fresh chives
>
> 1 tablespoon grated lemon peel
>
> 1 teaspoon Dijon mustard
>
> 1 teaspoon sugar

Mix all ingredients.

Beef Tenderloin
on Herb Biscuits

———— ✦ ————

Cook the beef and bake the biscuits in advance, then refrigerate beef. The day of the reception, assemble sandwiches. Serve Avocado Sauce on the side.

3 pounds beef tenderloin, trimmed
Herb Biscuits (below)
Avocado Sauce (right)

Heat oven to 400°. Place tenderloin on cookie sheet; tuck under narrow end. Bake 30 minutes; remove from cookie sheet. Cool; slice into ¼-inch slices. Prepare Herb Biscuits. Serve tenderloin slices on biscuits with Avocado Sauce.

About 40 sandwiches.

Herb Biscuits

1 cup margarine or butter
4 cups all-purpose flour
1 tablespoon sugar
2 tablespoons baking powder
½ teaspoon salt
2 cups milk
¼ cup chopped fresh or 2 tablespoons dried tarragon leaves

Heat oven to 450°. Cut margarine into flour, sugar, baking powder and salt with pastry blender until mixture resembles fine crumbs. Stir in milk and tarragon until dough leaves side of bowl. Drop by tablespoonfuls onto greased cookie sheet. Bake 10 to 12 minutes until golden brown. Immediately remove from cookie sheet.

Avocado Sauce

½ cup plain yogurt
1 tablespoon lemon juice
¼ teaspoon salt
1 medium ripe avocado, peeled and pitted

Place all ingredients in blender; cover and blend until smooth.

1 cup.

Fruit with Dip

———— ✦ ————

1 pound seedless green grapes, cut into small bunches
1 pound seedless red grapes, cut into small bunches
1 pint fresh blueberries
1 pint fresh raspberries
1 pint dark sweet cherries
1 pint Ranier, or other, cherries
1 honeydew, peeled and sliced
1 cantaloupe, peeled and sliced
1 cup sour cream
¼ cup packed brown sugar

Arrange fruit on large platter. Mix sour cream and brown sugar in small bowl; serve with fruit.

Lunch by the Water

Tarragon-Chicken Salad*

Marinated Tomato Slices*

French Bread

Lemonade Sorbet*

Blueberry Cupcakes*

Sparkling Water with Lime Slices

Serves 4

*S*ummer lunches are meant to be savored, and this lunch is perfect for lakeside lounging, poolside dining or easy eating anywhere on land or sea. You can make the Tarragon Chicken Salad and Marinated Tomato Slices ahead, then transport them to the waterside in coolers. If you are freezing sorbet in an ice-cream freezer, take the fixings along and make the sorbet by the water. Wherever you serve it, this lunch will go swimmingly!

THE FINISHING TOUCH

◆ Place a large, low glass bowl in center of the table and fill with water. Float flowers from your garden or the market in the water; spider mums and dahlias are good candidates. If you like, tint the water blue to continue the water theme.

◆ To make this luncheon special, wrap small gifts with metallic paper or foil and colored ribbon, and use the wrapped gifts to decorate the table. You can give gifts to your guests, or serve this as a birthday lunch.

◆ Choose a cool blue and white motif such as blue plates and napkins, a predominantly white tablecloth with a few bright spots of color and clear glass goblets.

◆ Play relaxing music, such as Handel's *Water Music*.

◆ The glare from water on a sunny day can give you quite a burn, almost before you know it. Have sunscreen on hand, and offer it to your guests.

Detail of centerpiece.

Tarragon-Chicken Salad

———— ◆ ————

This salad can be made the day before—just cover and refrigerate. Stir in honeydew balls just before serving.

> ½ cup mayonnaise
>
> ½ cup plain yogurt
>
> 2 tablespoons tarragon vinegar
>
> 1 tablespoon chopped fresh or 1 teaspoon dried tarragon leaves
>
> 4 cups cut-up cooked chicken
>
> 1 cup toasted, chopped pecans
>
> 2 cups honeydew balls
>
> Melon slices
>
> Lettuce

Mix mayonnaise, yogurt, vinegar and tarragon in large bowl; toss with chicken, pecans and honeydew. Serve salad on lettuce-lined plates with slices of melon.

Marinated Tomato Slices

———— ◆ ————

Cover the tomatoes and marinate in the refrigerator overnight for a richer flavor.

> ¼ cup chopped fresh or 2 tablespoons dried basil leaves
>
> 6 tablespoons olive oil
>
> 2 tablespoons red wine vinegar
>
> 2 large tomatoes, sliced

Mix all ingredients except tomatoes. Pour mixture over tomatoes in glass bowl; chill for at least 30 minutes.

Marinated Tomato Slices

Preceding page: A cooling tablecloth and clear glass complement Lunch by the Water.

Lemonade Sorbet

Sorbet can also be made in an ice-cream freezer. **Blend all ingredients and pour into ice-cream freezer; freeze according to manufacturer's directions.**

> *1½ cups cold water*
> *1 cup frozen lemonade concentrate*
> *3 tablespoons honey*

Place all ingredients in blender or food processor; cover and blend or process until smooth. Pour mixture into square baking dish, 8 × 8 × 2 inches. Freeze, stirring several times to keep mixture smooth, until firm. Garnish with lemon slices and blueberries if desired.

Lemonade Sorbet and Blueberry Cupcakes

Blueberry Cupcakes

> *1 cup all-purpose flour*
> *¾ cup sugar*
> *1 teaspoon baking powder*
> *½ teaspoon ground nutmeg*
> *½ cup sour cream*
> *¼ cup margarine or butter, melted*
> *1 egg, beaten*
> *1 cup blueberries*
> *Lemon Glaze (below)*

Heat oven to 350°. Line 12 medium muffin cups, 2½ × 1¼ inches, with paper baking cups. Mix flour, sugar, baking powder and nutmeg in large bowl. Stir in sour cream, margarine and egg just until moistened; fold in blueberries. Fill baking cups one-half full. Bake 25 to 30 minutes until wooden pick inserted in center comes out clean; cool. Spread about 1 teaspoon Lemon Glaze over each cupcake.

12 cupcakes.

Lemon Glaze

> *½ cup powdered sugar*
> *1 tablespoon lemon juice*
> *1 teaspoon grated lemon peel*

Mix all ingredients in small bowl.

Summer Clambake

Fresh Lemonade*

Clambake*

Sourdough Bread

Three Berry Cobbler*

Cold Watermelon

Cold Beer

Serves 12

Summer always seems better by the water; the ocean, a lake, a pool or even a sprink-
ler all add the delightful, cooling element of water. The clambake was invented to
make the best use of both the beach and summer's bounty in a combination that's easy,
casual and, most of all, fun. But even if you don't live near the beach, with our
complete instructions you can use your yard to create a fully satisfying, and delicious,
clambake of your own.

THE FINISHING TOUCH

◆ To prepare a clambake, dig a pit in dirt or
sand about twenty inches in diameter, and
be sure it's deep enough to hold eight inches
of charcoal. Light the charcoal and let it
burn for about thirty minutes, or until coals
are glowing. Secure a rack about two inches
from the coals on which to place the stockpot. If you are preparing this on a public
beach or in a park, check to be sure that

digging a pit and cooking will not be in
violation of any laws.

◆ Don't expect people to sit down formally
for this dinner—this is pure finger-food
fun, and guests may want to sit on the
beach, on the ground or at a table.

◆ Do be sure a table is available. A picnic
table is always a good choice, but if you
don't have one, or if one isn't provided at

the beach or park, bring along a few card tables from home. (Card tables seat four comfortably, so you'll need three to seat all twelve guests.)

✦ Create a whimsical clambake centerpiece by placing red paper flowers in a child's sand pail. Surround the pail with plastic glasses of water into which you have dropped "magic" clamshells that open and grow small scenes. (These are available in most novelty stores and stores that sell small toys.) Use inexpensive plastic toy lobsters and a few clamshells to fill in around the glasses.

✦ Buy paper lobster bibs to protect guests' clothing. Personalize the bibs by writing your own message with a marker. You can make a bib for each guest, using his or her name and some humorous reference, or make bibs with your name and a personal

statement, such as humorous "rules" for the clambake.

✦ For a beach clambake, bring along flashlights and insect repellent. Carry the cobbler in an airtight container to keep out the sand. Be sure to dig your pit well above the high-tide mark and to extinguish your fire thoroughly.

✦ For a backyard or park clambake, put out citronella candles to cut down on bugs. Check what time the park closes and be sure you have at least four hours for your clambake.

✦ Transport seafood in a cooler, to ensure food safety, then use the cooler to keep beverages chilled throughout the party.

✦ Play beach party music such as Jan and Dean, the Beach Boys or whatever makes you think of "sun and fun."

Fresh Lemonade

Tastes vary on the sweetness of lemonade, so feel free to adjust the sugar to your taste. You may want to make this on the tart side and let guests add sugar if they prefer it sweeter.

> *1 tablespoon grated lemon peel*
> *1½ cups sugar*
> *½ cup boiling water*
> *1½ cups lemon juice*
> *6 cups cold water*

Mix lemon peel, sugar and boiling water in 2-quart plastic or metal pitcher until sugar dissolves. Add lemon juice and cold water; stir. Serve with ice.

> *2 quarts.*

Traditionally clams were collected with a bucket and shovel, however, clams from a market are also delicious.

Clambake

✦

A 30- to 40-quart stockpot is a standard size in institutional kitchens, so you may be able to borrow one from your church kitchen or local school. If not, they are easy to rent.

12 ears of corn, unshucked
12 live lobsters (about 1 pound each)
3 pounds small white onions, peeled
3 pounds red potatoes, washed
4 pounds steamer clams, washed
Dill Butter (right)
Garlic-Lemon Butter (right)
Lemony Cocktail Sauce (right)

Prepare pit for clambake. Peel husks off corn; remove silk. Put 1 inch of water in a 30- to 40-quart stockpot. Place lobsters in pot, followed by onions, corn, potatoes and clams. Cover pot and place on rack in pit. Let water come to a boil (about 30 minutes). Cook with water boiling for 30 minutes or until potatoes are tender. Remove pot from fire; place food on large platters. Serve with sauces.

Dill Butter

2 cups margarine or butter, melted
¼ cup chopped fresh dill weed

Mix margarine and dill weed.

Garlic-Lemon Butter

2 cups margarine or butter, melted
2 tablespoons lemon juice
2 cloves garlic, crushed

Mix all ingredients.

Lemony Cocktail Sauce

½ lemon, seeded
¾ cup chili sauce
1 teaspoon prepared horseradish
1 clove garlic, crushed

Place lemon in food processor; process until finely ground. Stir in remaining ingredients. Refrigerate sauce in glass bowl.

Corn ready to be shucked for the clambake.

Three Berry Cobbler

———————◆———————

If you don't have fresh berries, you can substitute frozen berries. Use less sugar if frozen berries are slightly sweetened.

1½ *cups granulated sugar*

½ *cup cornstarch*

4 *cups fresh or frozen raspberries*

4 *cups fresh or frozen blueberries*

4 *cups fresh or frozen blackberries*

¼ *cup lemon juice*

1½ *cups all-purpose flour*

½ *cup packed brown sugar*

1½ *teaspoons baking powder*

½ *teaspoon salt*

½ *teaspoon ground nutmeg*

½ *cup margarine or butter*

⅓ *cup hot water*

Red, ripe watermelon makes the perfect dessert when paired with Three Berry Cobbler.

Heat oven to 400°. Grease 4-quart casserole. Mix granulated sugar and cornstarch in large bowl; sir in berries and lemon juice.

Combine remaining ingredients, except margarine and water, in large bowl. Blend margarine into flour mixture with pastry blender until mixture resembles coarse crumbs. Stir in hot water until mixture forms a soft dough. Spoon dough over berry mixture. Bake 35 to 45 minutes until topping is golden brown and fruit is slightly thickened. Serve with ice cream or cream if desired.

Fall

Tailgate Picnic

Hot Spiced Cider*

Pumpernickel Bagel Chips*

Tomato Soup with Dill*

Pita Sandwiches*

Gingerbread Cupcakes*

Fruit

Serves 4

T*he best football games include touchdowns for the home team and tailgate picnics for fans. Whether you are rooting for your high school, college, office or neighborhood team, don't forget to call "time-out" to enjoy this hearty fare.*

THE FINISHING TOUCH

◆ If serving from a station wagon, be sure to clean out the back of the car and vacuum it thoroughly before the picnic.

◆ It's still a tailgate picnic, even if you don't have a station wagon. Serve food on a picnic table, or if one isn't available, use the hood of the car.

◆ Cover tailgate, table or hood with a washable woven or braided cotton rug. Use your team's colors, if possible.

◆ Bring pretty, oversize paper napkins, and use them to line food baskets as well. Choose napkins that complement your rug.

◆ Bring an assortment of baskets, line with paper napkins, and place fruit, bagel chips, pita bread, dishes and silverware in them. Place baskets in a semicircle on serving area, with the largest basket in the center. Tie bows using your team's colors to basket handles.

Preceding pages: *Tailgate Picnic*

✦ Use heavy paper plates or simple plastic plates from home.
✦ Place a replica of the team mascot in the serving area, or add pennants, pompoms or a toy football painted in team colors.
✦ Bring hot cider and Tomato Soup with

Dill in thermos jugs with matching mugs. It's important to keep these foods hot, especially on a chilly fall afternoon.
✦ Bring along some folding chairs to sit on while you eat, and an afghan or blanket to ward off a chilly breeze.

Hot Spiced Cider

━━━━━◆━━━━━

10 cups apple cider
1 teaspoon whole cloves
½ teaspoon ground nutmeg
6 sticks cinnamon

Heat all ingredients to boiling in large saucepan over medium-high heat; reduce heat and simmer 10 minutes. Strain to remove whole spices. Keep hot.

Pumpernickel Bagel Chips

━━━━━◆━━━━━

These are perfect to float in Tomato Soup with Dill.

2 tablespoons vegetable oil
1 tablespoon margarine, melted
2 cloves garlic, crushed
3 pumpernickel or rye bagels, cut into ¼-inch slices

Heat oven to 325°. Mix oil, margarine and garlic; brush onto bagel slices. Bake slices on cookie sheet 10 to 12 minutes or until bagels are crisp. Store in tightly covered container.

12 bagel chips.

Tomato Soup with Dill

━━━━━◆━━━━━

3 tablespoons margarine or butter
2 medium onions, finely chopped (about 1 cup)
2 large carrots, peeled and finely chopped
2 cloves garlic, crushed
3 cups chicken broth
¾ teaspoon salt
½ teaspoon pepper
12 ripe medium tomatoes, seeded and diced (about 8 cups)
1 cup half-and-half
½ cup chopped fresh dill weed

Melt margarine in Dutch oven over medium heat. Cook and stir onions, carrots and garlic 5 minutes or until vegetables are soft. Add remaining ingredients except half-and-half and dill weed. Cook, uncovered, over medium heat 40 minutes, stirring occasionally. Cool slightly.

Place soup in blender or food processor; cover and blend or process until smooth. Stir in half-and-half. Keep soup hot until ready to serve. Serve with chopped dill weed.

Pita Sandwiches

———◆———

8 pita breads (6 inches in diameter)
½ pound cooked sliced turkey
½ pound cooked sliced roast beef
8 tomato slices
½ cup alfalfa sprouts
Peppery Mustard Sauce (below)
Horseradish Sauce (below)

Split each pita bread halfway around edge with knife; separate to form pocket. Place 2 slices turkey or roast beef in each pocket; top with tomato slice and sprouts. Serve sandwiches with Peppery Mustard Sauce and Horseradish Sauce.

8 sandwiches.

Peppery Mustard Sauce

¾ cup olive oil
3 tablespoons lemon juice
2 tablespoons grainy mustard
1 teaspoon cracked black pepper

Combine all ingredients in blender or food processor; cover and blend or process until smooth. Store tightly covered in refrigerator.

1¼ cups.

Horseradish Sauce

½ cup sour cream
2 tablespoons prepared horseradish
2 tablespoons apple cider

Mix all ingredients in small bowl. Refrigerate covered until chilled.

¾ cup.

Gingerbread Cupcakes

———◆———

1½ cups all-purpose flour
½ cup packed brown sugar
½ cup molasses
¼ cup margarine or butter, softened
1 teaspoon baking soda
2 teaspoons ground ginger
1 teaspoon ground cinnamon
½ teaspoon ground allspice
¼ teaspoon ground cloves
1 egg
¼ cup (2 ounces) cream cheese
Powdered sugar

Heat oven to 350°. Line 12 medium muffin cups, 2½ × 1¼ inches, with paper baking cups.

Beat all ingredients except cream cheese and powdered sugar in large bowl on low speed, scraping bowl constantly, 30 seconds. Beat on medium speed, scraping occasionally, 3 minutes. Spoon about 1 tablespoon dough into cups; top with 1 teaspoon cream cheese. Top with remaining dough to fill each cup one-half full.

Bake 20 to 22 minutes or until tops are dark golden brown. Let cupcakes cool. Sprinkle with powdered sugar.

12 cupcakes.

Garden Harvest Dinner

Corn Fritters*

Chicken in Red Wine Vinegar*

Caponata Lentil Salad*

Peach-Berry Clafouti*

Melon

Coffee and Tea

Serves 6

*F*or centuries, people have celebrated a successful harvest with a bountiful dinner. Even though most of us no longer live on farms, a harvest dinner is still a wonderful way to celebrate the fall season. Take a drive to admire the fall foliage, and keep an eye out for local produce stands to "harvest" the tomatoes, melons, herbs, corn, berries, peaches and eggplant in this menu. Of course, your local farmers' market or grocery store will also yield a "harvest" worthy of a celebration.

THE FINISHING TOUCH

- ◆ For a centerpiece, hollow out a large ornamental kale or savoy cabbage and fold back the leaves. Fill the cavity with tiny vegetables, such as carrots, green beans, squash, eggplant and cherry tomatoes. Use vegetables another day for a salad or in a stir-fry.
- ◆ Use a dark tablecloth in autumn colors— rust, brown, gold or dark green. Place contrasting napkins (in coordinating colors) in the unfilled water glasses.

- ◆ Use small eggplants at each place to hold name cards. Cut a slit into the top of the eggplant, then place a hand-lettered card into slot. (See photo on page 87.)
- ◆ Decorate the table with ropes of grape vines. String together garlic cloves, dried peppers, small gourds, tiny squashes, Indian corn or other available fall produce and twine through the vines. Make some short strings for guests to take home. Loop strings

across the kitchen or dining room ceiling until time to distribute them to guests.

✦ If possible, serve this dinner outside—a barn is the perfect setting. Place the dishes on an old hay wagon or create a simple trestle table. Sit on bales of hay, if available, or bring out chairs.

✦ Tie cornstalks with wide ribbon to harmonize with the tablecloth and napkins, and decorate the wagon with them. If eating inside, decorate the dining room with the corn stalks.

✦ Use a blackboard to write out your menu for a country, "farmer's market" feel.

✦ Make a scarecrow out of old clothes and two pieces of wood nailed together in the form of a lowercase *t*. Add a hat, and straw or rope hair. Make a simple face, and let the scarecrow perch on the wagon or guard the dining room from a comfortable perch. This is a fun project for children.

Corn Fritters

◆

Vegetable oil

1 cup all-purpose flour

½ cup milk

1 tablespoon chopped fresh or 1 teaspoon dried basil leaves

1 teaspoon baking powder

1 teaspoon vegetable oil

¼ teaspoon salt

¼ teaspoon pepper

2 eggs

1 cup whole kernel corn

Heat oil (1 inch) in deep fryer or Dutch oven to 375°. Beat remaining ingredients except corn until smooth; stir in corn. Drop by tablespoonfuls into hot oil. Fry about 5 minutes or until completely cooked; drain.

Opposite: *Chicken in Red Wine Vinegar and Peach-Berry Clafouti.* Above left: *Small eggplants hold name cards* (see page 85); above right: *Detail of vegetable centerpiece* (see page 85).

Chicken in Red Wine Vinegar

◆

2 tablespoons margarine or butter

2 cloves garlic, crushed

3 shallots, chopped

6 boneless skinless chicken breast halves (about 2¼ pounds)

½ cup red wine vinegar

2 cups finely chopped tomato (about 2 medium tomatoes)

2 teaspoons chopped fresh or ½ teaspoon dried thyme leaves

½ teaspoon salt

¼ teaspoon pepper

Melt margarine in 10-inch skillet. Add garlic, shallots and chicken. Cook over medium-high heat 12 to 15 minutes, turning after 6 minutes, until chicken is no longer pink. Reduce heat to low. Add vinegar; cover and cook 5 minutes. Stir in remaining ingredients, turn chicken. Cook over low heat 10 to 12 minutes until chicken is done.

GARDEN HARVEST
DINNER

- Lentil Caponata Salad
- CHICKEN Breasts
- Corn fritters
- Melon w/ Garden Herbs
- Peach Clafouti

Caponata Lentil Salad

◆

Caponata is a Sicilian vegetable specialty made with tomatoes and eggplant and usually served at room temperature. Italians serve caponata as a first course or accompaniment to the main course.

½ cup lentils, rinsed

¼ cup olive oil

1 medium onion, finely chopped (about ½ cup)

1 medium eggplant, diced (about 2 cups)

¼ cup white wine vinegar

2 tablespoons currants

1 tablespoon chopped fresh or 1 teaspoon dried basil leaves

1 tablespoon chopped fresh parsley

1 teaspoon sugar

½ teaspoon salt

¼ teaspoon pepper

1 medium tomato, chopped (about ¾ cup)

1 small red bell pepper, chopped (about ½ cup)

Cover lentils with water in medium saucepan. Cover; heat to boiling over medium-high heat. Reduce heat and simmer 15 minutes. Drain; cool in large bowl.

Heat oil in 10-inch skillet; add onion and cook 2 to 3 minutes until softened. Add eggplant; cook 5 to 8 minutes, stirring frequently, until eggplant is tender. Blend eggplant mixture with lentils in large bowl. Add remaining ingredients to skillet. Cook over low heat 10 to 15 minutes until liquid has evaporated.

Combine tomato mixture with lentil mixture. Cover and refrigerate 1 to 2 hours to blend flavors. Serve on lettuce leaves if desired.

Peach-Berry Clafouti

◆

4 peaches, pared, pitted and sliced

½ cup blackberries or blueberries

1½ cups milk

¾ cup all-purpose flour

½ cup sugar

½ teaspoon ground nutmeg

2 eggs

Heat oven to 350°. Grease quiche dish, 10 × 1½ inches. Arrange peaches and berries in bottom of dish.

Place remaining ingredients in blender or food processor; cover and blend or process until smooth. Carefully pour batter over fruit. Bake 45 to 55 minutes or until top is golden brown and center is set.

Cool 10 minutes; cut into wedges. Serve warm with whipped cream if desired.

Preceding pages: *Garden Harvest Dinner served on a hay wagon.*

Columbus Day Luncheon

Italian Vegetable Soup*

Antipasto Salad*

Herb Foccacia*

Pear-Plum Compote*

Biscotti

Cappuccino

Serves 6

Although Christopher Columbus did not "discover" America—it had many thriving cultures centuries before his voyage—he did open trade and immigration routes from Europe to the Americas. Columbus Day celebrates his contribution to the history of the Americas, and this luncheon honors Columbus's Italian heritage.

THE FINISHING TOUCH

- Use a globe as a centerpiece. Surround it with three toy sailboats representing Columbus's ships—the *Nina*, the *Pinta* and the *Santa Maria*.
- Locate reproductions of old maps dating from the end of the fifteenth century when Columbus made his first voyage, and cut to form placemats. Or find one reproduction and photocopy it to make placemats. You can also buy laminated map place mats of any geographical region, perhaps one that shows your hometown.
- Set out informal, homespun napkins.
- Use Italian pottery dishes and a few terra-cotta serving pieces.
- Place a small plastic dragon or a fanciful monster at each place to represent the monsters fifteenth-century sailors believed to inhabit the seas.
- Lead the way into the dining room with signs saying, "This way to the Orient." Columbus originally intended to prove the world was round, and Queen Isabella of Spain financed his trip to open trade routes to the Orient. They were both surprised when he bumped into America!

Italian Vegetable Soup

——◆——

1 medium onion, finely chopped (about ½ cup)

1 clove garlic, crushed

2 tablespoons olive oil

2 medium zucchini, diced (about 2 cups)

2 medium yellow squash, diced (about 2 cups)

1 small yellow bell pepper, chopped (about ½ cup)

½ cup chopped fresh or 2 tablespoons dried basil leaves

½ teaspoon salt

¼ teaspoon pepper

4½ cups chicken broth

1 cup Italian Arborio or short grain rice

1 can (28 ounces) Italian plum tomatoes, chopped

Grated Parmesan cheese

Cook onion and garlic over medium heat in oil in Dutch oven until softened. Stir in zucchini, squash, bell pepper, basil, salt and pepper. Cook over medium heat, stirring frequently, about 8 minutes until vegetables are crisp-tender. Add remaining ingredients except Parmesan cheese. Heat mixture to boiling over medium-high heat, stirring occasionally. Cover; reduce heat to medium-low. Simmer 25 to 30 minutes until rice is tender. Serve with Parmesan cheese.

Antipasto Salad

——◆——

Have fun choosing different sausages, cheeses, olives and peppers for this salad. Look for different varieties at a neighborhood Italian market, specialty store or deli.

¼ cup Italian olives

8 ounces fresh mozzarella cheese, drained and cubed

4 ounces sliced Italian salami

4 ounces sliced Italian capicolla, prosciutto, or fully cooked smoked Virginia ham

4 ounces marinated Italian peppers

1 jar (8 ounces) marinated mushrooms, drained

¼ cup chopped fresh basil leaves

Vinaigrette (below)

Arrange all ingredients except basil on 6 salad plates. Sprinkle with fresh basil. Serve with Vinaigrette.

Vinaigrette

⅓ cup olive oil

3 tablespoons red wine vinegar

1 clove garlic, crushed

Mix all ingredients.

Herb Foccacia

———◆———

Make this traditional Italian bread the day before your luncheon and warm before serving.

2 packages active dry yeast

¼ teaspoon sugar

1 cup warm water

3 cups all-purpose flour

¼ cup finely chopped onion

3 tablespoons vegetable oil

1 teaspoon salt

Herb Glaze (below)

Mix yeast, sugar and water in small bowl; let stand 5 minutes.

Blend remaining ingredients except Herb Glaze in large bowl; stir in yeast mixture to form a soft dough. Turn dough out onto floured surface. Knead dough 5 minutes until smooth and elastic. Place dough in greased bowl; cover and let rise in warm place 1 hour.

Grease baking sheet. Punch dough down; divide evenly into 6 pieces. Shape each piece into 5-inch circle; place on baking sheet. Cover; let rise 20 minutes.

Heat oven to 400°. Brush top of each bread with Herb Glaze. Bake 15 to 18 minutes until light golden brown.

6 foccacia.

Herb Glaze

1 tablespoon chopped fresh or ½ teaspoon dried thyme leaves

1 tablespoon chopped fresh or ½ teaspoon dried basil leaves

1 egg, beaten

Mix all ingredients.

Pear-Plum Compote

———◆———

Serve Biscotti—simple Italian cookies—with the compote. Biscotti can be found in Italian markets, specialty stores and many supermarkets.

1 cup dry white wine or white grape juice

1 cup water

½ cup sugar

2 tablespoons grated orange peel

10 plums, pitted and cut into fourths

4 large pears, peeled, cored and sliced

Plain yogurt

Combine all ingredients except yogurt in large nonmetal saucepan. Heat to boiling; cover and reduce heat to low. Simmer 10 minutes or until fruit is tender. Let mixture cool. Serve with dollops of yogurt.

Halloween Breakfast

Papaya-Orange Juice*

Twisted Bacon*

Surprise French Toast*

Fruit in a Minipumpkin*

Serves 4

*H*alloween night begins early, and with candy to come, a Halloween dinner does not get much attention from kids. However, starting off Halloween morning with this fun breakfast gets kids in the mood for a whole day of "thrills and chills." This meal is also good to serve on the weekend before Halloween. Invite your children's friends over or host a breakfast for other young friends—even adults who are still kids at heart.

————— THE FINISHING TOUCH —————

◆ Use your jack-o'-lantern as a centerpiece. Ask children to help carve the pumpkin the day before.

◆ Stick a dead branch, without leaves, into an orange to serve as an anchor. Cut out tiny pumpkins, ghosts, bats, witches and so on from colored paper and hang the decorations on the branch. Add the tree to the jack-o'-lantern centerpiece. This is an excellent project for children.

◆ Use a black marker and draw faces on the miniature pumpkins for the fruit salad. If you like, decorate a few more pumpkins than you need to serve, and add them to the centerpiece. This is another great project for children.

◆ Use a black and white plaid or checked tablecloth. Buy orange and black paper plates and napkins.

◆ If you don't want to use a tablecloth, try decorated trick-or-treat bags as place mats or make your own from little brown paper bags.

◆ Put a trick-or-treat bag at each place. Paint and decorate brown paper bags with favorite Halloween fiends, friends or familiars.

◆ Kids aren't the only ones who get to play tricks at Halloween. Hide a plastic spider or other Halloween joke item under the plates, or balance one on a serving platter.

◆ If it's a weekend, rent a scary film to view after breakfast. In the daylight you won't have to worry about the lights going off!

Halloween Breakfast—a great start to a scary day.

Trick or treat bags.

Papaya-Orange Juice

━━━━━◆━━━━━

3 cups orange juice

2 tablespoons honey

1 large ripe papaya, peeled, seeded and chopped

4 orange slices

Place all ingredients except orange slices in blender; cover and blend until smooth. Divide mixture among 4 glasses; top with orange slice.

Twisted Bacon

━━━━━◆━━━━━

8 slices bacon

Heat oven to 400°. Twist bacon slices tightly; place slices on rack in broiler pan. Bake, without turning, about 10 minutes until brown; drain.

Surprise French Toast

━━━━━◆━━━━━

Use jams, jellies or peanut butter as a "surprise" in your French toast, along with the cream cheese in the recipe.

1 package (3 ounces) cream cheese

16 slices (½ inch thick) French bread

1 cup milk

4 eggs

2 tablespoons margarine or butter

Powdered sugar

Syrup

Spread 1 tablespoon cream cheese on each of 8 slices bread; top with second slice bread. Whisk together milk and eggs in large bowl.

Heat griddle or large skillet over medium heat or to 350°; melt margarine. Dip sandwiches in egg mixture; carefully place on griddle. Cook about 8 minutes on a side until golden brown. Sprinkle with powdered sugar; serve with syrup.

4 servings (2 sandwiches each).

Homemade Halloween tree (see page 94).

Fruit in a Minipumpkin

———◆———

Cut a 4-inch opening in top of each pumpkin. Scoop out seeds. Mix bananas and peaches; fill each pumpkin with about ¼ cup fruit.

You can add other fruits to this recipe to make it just the way your kids or guests will like it.

> *4 miniature pumpkins*
> *2 bananas, sliced*
> *1 can (16 ounces) sliced peaches, drained*

Fruit in a Minipumpkin and Papaya-Orange Juice

French Country Picnic

Mustard Steak on Baguettes*

Celery Root Salad*

White Bean Salad*

Brown Sugar Tart*

Cider

Serves 8

*P*icnics range from simple to sophisticated, and this menu combines country charm with continental flair. A hike in the country will work up an appetite for a good lunch, and you'll be able to feed a crowd as well as gather compliments for this unusual, and unusually appealing, picnic.

THE FINISHING TOUCH

◆ Along your hike stop to gather branches with colorful fall leaves, lichens, mosses, attractive stones, mushrooms and so on to decorate the picnic table.

◆ Pack a glass canning jar in which to place the branches you gather. Wrap napkins around the jar and place a few inside so they take up less space in the picnic basket as well as to prevent breakage.

◆ Bring a washable cotton rug or blanket for a tablecloth. If you choose to sit on the ground, use the rug or blanket to sit on and make into your "table."

◆ Use large napkins in a French provincial or other small print.

◆ Pack French sparkling water in your thermos, or bring along sparkling French cider instead of regular cider.

◆ Sing your favorite French songs during the picnic to set the mood. Try "On the Bridge at Avignon" or "Frère Jacques" or your Maurice Chevalier impersonation of "Thank Heaven for Little Girls." This may be a bit corny, but it can also be fun.

Mustard Steak on Baguettes

———————◆———————

Pack the meat and baguettes separately, and assemble the sandwiches only when you are ready to eat, so the bread doesn't get soggy.

> 2 beef top round steaks (1½ pounds each)
>
> ¼ cup Dijon mustard
>
> 2 tablespoons sweet paprika
>
> 1 tablespoon cracked black peppercorns
>
> 1 tablespoon chopped fresh or 1 teaspoon dried thyme leaves
>
> 1 teaspoon ground red pepper (cayenne)
>
> 8 individual baguettes

Trim fat from beef steak. Cut both sides of beef into diamond pattern ⅛ inch deep. Place in shallow 2-quart glass dish. Mix remaining ingredients, except baguettes; spread on both sides of steak. Cover and refrigerate overnight.

Remove beef from dish. Brush broiler pan rack with vegetable oil. Place steaks on rack in pan. Broil with top 4 inches from heat, 12 to 14 minutes, turning once, until desired doneness. Cut diagonally into thin slices; serve on baguettes.

Celery Root Salad

———————◆———————

Celery root is the root of the celery plant, not the stalk. It should be peeled before shredding and marinating. Make this salad the night before the hike, so you can get off to an early start.

> ¾ cup plain yogurt
>
> ¼ cup mayonnaise
>
> 1 tablespoon prepared horseradish
>
> 2 teaspoons Dijon mustard
>
> 4 cups shredded celery root (about 2 pounds)

Stir all ingredients except celery root in medium bowl until well blended; add celery root. Cover tightly; refrigerate 1 to 2 hours to blend flavors. (As celery root marinates in dressing, it becomes tender.)

Above: Autumn's bounty is a lovely backdrop for a picnic.

White Bean Salad

———— ◆ ————

This is also best made the night before. Stir in walnuts just before serving.

- ¼ cup olive oil
- 3 tablespoons lemon juice
- ½ teaspoon pepper
- ¼ teaspoon salt
- ¼ cup chopped fresh parsley
- 3 green onions (with tops), sliced
- 1 small red bell pepper, chopped
- 2 cans (16 ounces each) great northern beans, drained
- ½ cup chopped walnuts

Combine oil, lemon juice, pepper and salt in medium bowl until well blended. Add remaining ingredients except walnuts; stir to coat. Cover and refrigerate at least 1 hour. Stir in walnuts.

Brown Sugar Tart

———— ◆ ————

- ¾ cup margarine or butter
- 2¼ cups firmly packed brown sugar
- 1 tablespoon vanilla
- 2 eggs
- 2 cups all-purpose flour
- 1½ teaspoons baking powder
- 1 cup chopped walnuts
- 1 cup semisweet chocolate chips, melted

Heat oven to 350°. Grease springform pan, 10 × 2 inches. Heat margarine and brown sugar in medium saucepan 5 minutes or until margarine melts; remove from heat. Beat in vanilla and eggs. Add flour and baking powder; stir until well blended. Stir in nuts.

Pour mixture into pan. Bake 35 to 45 minutes until golden brown and set in center; cool. Remove sides of springform pan. Drizzle top of tart with melted chocolate; cut into wedges.

Apple Harvest Dinner

Chicken-Apple Terrine*

Fruit-stuffed Pork Roast*

Pear and Blue Cheese Salad*

Sautéed Spinach*

Crispy Potato Pancakes*

Glazed Apple-Plum Cake*

Serves 8

Picking *apples in the fall is a true pleasure; the brisk air, the sweet scent of the apples and the welcome exercise of filling your basket make the experience memorable. About the only thing better is your first bite of a crisp, juicy, newly picked apple. This menu is perfect after a day of apple picking and features apples in unusual and delicious ways. Try different types of apples for a variety of flavors. One of these recipes may well become the new culinary apple of your eye!*

THE FINISHING TOUCH

◆ Investigate local orchards where you can pick apples, and invite a group of friends to go apple picking. Come home to this dinner, or plan dinner for the following day if you want to use the apples you picked at the orchard.

◆ As a centerpiece, use a large bowl, rectangular vegetable basket or round basket piled high with assorted apples. Try to vary the sizes and colors—mix together red, yellow and green apples and tuck crabapples and acorns in and around the apples.

◆ Place apple-shaped candles around the centerpiece. If you don't want to buy specially shaped candles, core several apples and place a three-inch white candle in each apple.

◆ Use dark red woven place mats, and look for paper napkins printed with apples, or use red and brown cloth napkins.

- ✦ Buy a few apple botanical prints; inexpensive reproductions are available at picture shops and some art galleries and museum shops. Place them on the table in the most pleasing configuration, such as down the center, or around the centerpiece. If food is likely to come in contact with the prints, cover with a piece of plastic wrap. You may want to buy a frame for one or two prints—they are particularly attractive in a kitchen.
- ✦ Put small wreaths at each place, or make strings of dried apples of each place.
- ✦ Buy one or two serving pieces with an apple design, such as salt and pepper shakers, a pitcher, a platter or a bowl.
- ✦ Bob for apples, either before or after dinner, whichever suits your schedule best.
- ✦ Give guests their own bag of apples to take home.
- ✦ Cut a small apple or crabapple in half; press onto ink pad. Print apple pattern on bags to fill with apples to give to guests.

Chicken-Apple Terrine

A "terrine" takes its name from the type of dish in which it's baked. This terrine is meant to be served in slices as a first course. You can also serve it on bread or crackers as an appetizer before dinner.

> 1 medium green apple, peeled, cored and thinly sliced
>
> 1½ pounds skinless boneless chicken breasts, cut into 1-inch pieces
>
> ¼ cup apple brandy or apple cider
>
> 1 tablespoon all-purpose flour
>
> 1 teaspoon salt
>
> ½ teaspoon ground nutmeg
>
> ¼ teaspoon ground allspice
>
> 2 shallots, peeled
>
> 2 eggs
>
> 1 cup chopped green apple

Heat oven to 350°. Grease a 4-cup porcelain terrine or glass mold. Arrange apple slices on bottom of terrine. Place chicken in food processor; cover and process until coarsely ground. Add remaining ingredients except chopped apple. Cover and process until smooth. Stir in chopped apple.

Spread mixture in terrine; cover tightly. Bake 60 to 70 minutes until meat thermometer inserted in center registers 180°. Let stand 1 hour. Refrigerate at least 3 hours. Uncover; invert into serving platter. Remove terrine; garnish with additional apple slices if desired.

Fruit-stuffed Pork Roast

Fruit-stuffed Pork Roast

————◆————

3 pounds boneless pork loin roast

1 cup pitted prunes, chopped

1 cup chopped tart apple

2 tablespoons dry bread crumbs

2 teaspoons chopped fresh or ½ teaspoon dried rosemary leaves

¼ teaspoon salt

1 cup apple brandy or apple cider

Apple Brandy Sauce (right)

Heat oven to 350°. Starting at narrow side of pork roast, cut a slit lengthwise almost to center of roast. (Roast will open like a book.) Mix remaining ingredients except brandy and Apple Brandy Sauce. Stuff mixture into opening; close and secure with string.

Pour brandy into roasting pan; place stuffed roast into pan. Bake 1 to 1½ hours, basting frequently with brandy, until meat thermometer inserted in center registers 160°. Serve pork with Apple Brandy Sauce.

Apple Brandy Sauce

1 cup apple cider

¼ cup apple brandy or apple cider

2 teaspoons cornstarch

Mix all ingredients in small saucepan. Heat to boiling, stirring constantly. Boil and stir 1 minute until sauce thickens slightly.

1¼ cups.

Following pages: *Apple Harvest Dinner served as a buffet.*

Pear and Blue Cheese Salad

————————◆————————

Romaine lettuce leaves

2 red pears, cored and thinly sliced

2 green pears, cored and thinly sliced

½ cup crumbled blue cheese

Cider Vinaigrette (below)

Arrange lettuce leaves on each of 8 salad plates. Divide red and green pear slices evenly among plates; top each salad with about 1 tablespoon blue cheese. Drizzle each salad with about 2 tablespoons Cider Vinaigrette.

Cider Vinaigrette

½ cup light olive oil or vegetable oil

2 tablespoons cider vinegar

1 teaspoon Dijon mustard

¼ teaspoon salt

¼ teaspoon pepper

Shake all ingredients in tightly covered container.

Sautéed Spinach

————————◆————————

¼ cup margarine or butter

1½ pounds fresh spinach, washed and drained

¾ teaspoon ground nutmeg

½ teaspoon salt

Melt margarine in large skillet; add remaining ingredients. Cook and stir 5 minutes until spinach is wilted. Serve immediately.

Crispy Potato Pancakes

————————◆————————

4 large baking potatoes (about 1 pound), peeled and shredded

½ cup beer or milk

¼ cup all-purpose flour

¼ cup finely chopped onion

2 tablespoons finely chopped parsley

½ teaspoon salt

¼ teaspoon pepper

1 egg

2 to 3 tablespoons vegetable oil

Mix all ingredients except oil until well blended. Heat oil on griddle or in large skillet until hot. Spread about ¼ cup batter on griddle for each pancake. Cook on medium-high heat 2 minutes on each side until crispy; keep warm. Add more oil to griddle, if necessary. Serve with applesauce if desired.

12 pancakes.

Basket of fresh apples with personalized guest bags.

Glazed Apple Plum Cake

————◆————

1 cup packed brown sugar

½ cup margarine or butter

1 cup applesauce

1 egg

2½ cups all-purpose flour

2 teaspoons baking soda

1 teaspoon cinnamon

½ teaspoon ground nutmeg

¼ teaspoon ground cloves

1 can (16½ ounces) purple plums, drained and chopped

2 tart cooking apples, peeled, cored and cut in half lengthwise

¼ cup plum jam, melted

Glazed Apple Plum Cake

Heat oven to 350°. Grease springform pan, 9 × 3 inches. Beat brown sugar and margarine in large bowl until light and fluffy; mix in applesauce and egg. Blend flour, baking soda, cinnamon, nutmeg and cloves into margarine mixture. Stir in plums. Spoon batter into pan. Slice apples crosswise into thin slices. Arrange apple slices decoratively in batter. Bake 55 to 65 minutes until wooden pick inserted in center comes out clean. Brush top of cake with plum jam. Let cake cool in pan 20 minutes; remove sides. Serve warm, with ice cream if desired.

About 16 slices.

Thanksgiving Dinner

Scalloped Sweet Potatoes*

Turkey with Apricot–Wild Rice Stuffing*

Mashed Potatoes

Cranberry-Raspberry Salad*

Vegetables with Lemon Butter*

Lettuce Salad with Balsamic Vinaigrette*

Pumpkin Cheesecake*

Chilled Cranberry Juice

Coffee and Tea

Serves 12

Gathering friends and family to celebrate Thanksgiving is a wonderful annual event. However, planning a menu that includes everyone's traditional favorites as well as some new ideas can be a real challenge. Our generous menu for twelve features the classic turkey, but with an exciting and different stuffing, while our Scalloped Sweet Potatoes may convert people who always thought they disliked sweet potatoes. The Pumpkin Cheesecake is a marvelous twist on pumpkin pie and may well become your dessert of choice for future Thanksgiving dinners. For this meal, bounty is the watchword, so our menu has room for your family's mashed potato recipe, a second dessert and any other favorite recipes that you would like to include in your celebration of the day.

———— THE FINISHING TOUCH ————

◆ To make Thanksgiving a celebration, not a chore, ask guests and family members to bring a dish. They can make their specialties, which can be added to the menu, or you can assign each person a dish from this menu and provide the recipe.

◆ Most dining room tables aren't large enough for twelve, and there are various ways to serve a large group. If your table has leaves, add enough to seat twelve. You may want to remove furniture from the dining room to accommodate the table. You can also seat as many people as possible at your table, then set up card tables close by. Or you may want to remove your regular table and group card tables in the dining room.

◆ Bring out your largest soup tureen or vegetable dish to use as a vase for a large bouquet of chrysanthemums. Mix various shades, highlighting autumn colors. If serving at several tables, make smaller-scale bouquets, using an assortment of pretty vases or pitchers.

◆ Surround the centerpiece with brass candlesticks, using candles that match the fall colors of the flowers. Light the candles just before you serve dinner.

◆ Use a linen tablecloth, or cloths, and napkins that match the autumn colors in the tablecloth.

◆ Serve on your best china, and use your nicest tableware. Amber stemware and dessert plates carry through the autumn theme nicely.

◆ Place a colorful, pressed leaf under each water glass as a "coaster."

◆ Tie a bronze or yellow chrysanthemum to each napkin with a gold ribbon.

Scalloped Sweet Potatoes

————◆————

3½ *pounds sweet potatoes, peeled and thinly sliced*

4½ *cups half-and-half*

½ *teaspoon salt*

¼ *teaspoon white pepper*

1 *cup packed brown sugar*

½ *teaspoon ground nutmeg*

Heat oven to 350°. Grease rectangular baking dish, 13 × 9 × 2 inches. Heat sweet potatoes and half-and-half to boiling in large saucepan; cook 1 minute, stirring frequently. Stir in salt and pepper.

Spoon mixture into baking dish. Cover and bake 45 minutes. Uncover; sprinkle top with brown sugar and nutmeg. Bake mixture 10 minutes or until top is golden brown.

Turkey with Apricot–Wild Rice Stuffing

———— ◆ ————

Apricot–Wild Rice Stuffing (right)
18- to 20-pound turkey
Margarine or butter, melted
1 cup cranberry-apricot juice

Prepare Apricot–Wild Rice Stuffing. Fill wishbone area of turkey with stuffing. Fasten neck skin to back with skewer. Fold wings across back with tips touching. Fill body cavity lightly. (Do not pack—stuffing will expand.) Tuck drumsticks under band of skin at tail, or skewer to tail.

Spoon any remaining stuffing into ungreased casserole; cover. (Refrigerate until about 30 minutes before turkey is done. Bake covered at 325° until hot, about 45 minutes.)

Heat oven to 325°. Place turkey, breast side up, on rack in shallow pan. Brush with margarine. Insert meat thermometer so tip is in thickest part of thigh muscle or thickest part of breast and does not touch bone. (Tip of thermometer can be inserted in center of stuffing.) Do not add water. Do not cover. Roast until done, 5½ to 6½ hours.

Place a tent of aluminum foil loosely over turkey when it begins to turn golden. After 2½ hours, cut band or remove skewer holding legs. Baste turkey with cranberry-apricot juice during last 2 hours of roasting. Turkey is done when thermometer placed in thigh or breast registers 185°. (Thermometer inserted in stuffing will register 165°.)

Let stand about 20 minutes before carving. As soon as possible after serving, remove stuffing from turkey. Refrigerate stuffing and turkey separately, and use within 2 days.

Apricot–Wild Rice Stuffing

2½ cups hot water
2 cups cooked wild rice
1 cup chopped, toasted pecans
½ cup margarine or butter, melted
1 large onion, chopped (about 1 cup)
1 package (16 ounces) herb stuffing mix
1 package (11 ounces) dried apricots, chopped

Mix all ingredients in deep bowl. Stir to blend well.

Cranberry-Raspberry Salad

———— ◆ ————

2 packages (12 ounces each) cranberry-orange sauce
1 package (12 ounces) cranberry-raspberry sauce
1 package (6 ounces) lemon gelatin
2 cups boiling water

Lightly oil 6½-cup ring mold. Mix cranberry sauces together in large bowl. Dissolve gelatin in boiling water; stir into cranberry sauces. Pour into mold. Cover and refrigerate overnight.

Unmold salad. Garnish with watercress and cranberries if desired.

Vegetables
with Lemon Butter

———◆———

3 packages (10 ounces each) frozen whole green beans

1½ pounds Brussels sprouts, cut into halves

1 pound carrots, peeled and cut into julienne strips

½ cup margarine or butter, melted

1 tablespoon grated lemon peel

1 tablespoon lemon juice

Cook green beans according to package directions; keep warm.

Heat 1 inch water to boiling in large saucepan. Add Brussels sprouts. Cover and heat to boiling; reduce heat. Cook 8 to 10 minutes or until stems are tender; keep warm.

Heat 1 inch water to boiling in large saucepan. Add carrots. Cover and heat to boiling; reduce heat. Cook 6 to 8 minutes or until tender; keep warm.

Combine margarine, lemon peel and lemon juice. Arrange cooked vegetables on platter; pour margarine mixture over vegetables.

Lettuce Salad
with Balsamic Vinaigrette

———◆———

Balsamic Vinaigrette (below)

1 head leaf lettuce, torn into bite-size pieces

1 head escarole, torn into bite-size pieces

1 cup finely chopped red onion

4 seedless oranges, peeled and thinly sliced

Mix lettuces and onion in large serving bowl; top with orange slices. Toss with Balsamic Vinaigrette.

Balsamic Vinaigrette

3 tablespoons lemon juice

1 tablespoon balsamic vinegar

2 teaspoons Dijon mustard

1 clove garlic, crushed

½ cup olive oil

Combine all ingredients except oil; slowly whisk in oil until well blended.

Pumpkin Cheesecake

———— ♦ ————

1½ cups graham cracker crumbs

½ cup finely chopped pecans

⅓ cup packed brown sugar

½ cup margarine or butter, melted

3 packages (8 ounces each) cream cheese, softened

½ cup sour cream

1 cup packed brown sugar

2 teaspoons ground cinnamon

½ teaspoon ground nutmeg

½ teaspoon ground ginger

¼ teaspoon ground allspice

1 can (16 ounces) pumpkin

3 eggs

Caramelized Sugar (right)

Mix graham cracker crumbs, pecans, ⅓ cup brown sugar and the margarine. Press evenly on bottom and sides of ungreased springform pan, 9 × 3 inches. Refrigerate 20 minutes.

Heat oven to 300°. Beat cream cheese, sour cream, 1 cup brown sugar and the spices in large bowl on medium speed until smooth. Add pumpkin. Beat in eggs on low speed. Pour over crumb mixture. Bake about 1¼ hours or until center is firm. Cover and refrigerate at least 3 hours but no longer than 48 hours.

Prepare Caramelized Sugar; drizzle with fork over top of chilled cheesecake. Loosen cheesecake from side of pan; remove side of pan. Place cheesecake on plate. Refrigerate any remaining cheesecake immediately.

Caramelized Sugar

1 cup sugar

3 tablespoons water

Combine sugar and water in small saucepan. Boil mixture over medium heat, stirring until sugar is dissolved. Boil syrup, without stirring, until golden brown. Remove from heat and gently swirl until syrup stops cooking. Let caramel cool about 1 minute or until thick enough to drizzle from fork.

Fall Game Dinner

Rock Cornish Hens with Sour Cherry Sauce*

Roasted Autumn Vegetables*

Wild Mushroom Risotto*

Salad with Hot Cider Dressing*

Pumpkin Bread Pudding*

Serves 4

*F*all is the time to enjoy game, and if you are lucky enough to have easy access to fresh pheasant, do use it in this dinner. However, the Rock Cornish hens are also excellent and are still reminiscent of the early days of the country when bringing home game was a fall treat.

THE FINISHING TOUCH

♦ For a centerpiece, fill a shallow bowl with branches of fall berries, such as elderberries, rose hips and bittersweet. Add some chrysanthemums to the arrangement for balance and color. If you have a duck decoy, use it as a centerpiece, and place berries around it.

♦ Buy inexpensive fabric with a feather design, and use it as a runner down the middle of your table. (A yard of fabric is plenty for a runner.) Or, cut a square for the center of the table. (Half a yard is more than enough for a square—you may want to look in the store's remnant section for an even smaller piece of fabric.) Tuck a few feathers into the centerpiece.

♦ Set out cloth napkins in solid colors that coordinate with your fabric.

♦ Paint apples, pears, grapes or flowers on linen napkins using permanent dyes or acrylic paints. Thin paints if necessary to get the look of watercolors.

♦ Make swags to decorate the center of the table using bunches of raffia. Divide the raffia into three 2-inch-diameter bunches, about fifty inches long. Braid the raffia, leaving about six inches loose at both ends and tie with bows. Fold the braided raffia in half and secure at top. Glue dried flowers, dried peppers, garlic, dried herbs and so forth to the braid. Tie the raffia into a bow at the top of the braid. Lay braid flat on center of table to decorate.

✦ As an alternative to decorating your table with fabric, use an inexpensive wallpaper border pattern of game, such as ducks, geese or pheasant. Cut the paper into two runners on either side of the table, or use as a square in the center.

✦ Look for inexpensive game prints and hang them in the dining room for the evening. If you don't plan to hang prints in the house permanently, "borrow" frames from other pictures in the house, and frame the prints for the evening. You can also prop prints, unframed, on the sideboard, tea cart, hutch or other dining room furniture.

✦ If you like puns, plan on playing a board or card game after dinner. Then you will truly have a "game" dinner!

Dinner plate with servings of Rock Cornish Game Hen with Sour Cherry Sauce, Roasted Autumn Vegetables and Wild Mushroom Risotto.

Rock Cornish Hens
with Sour Cherry Sauce

———————◆———————

2 lemons, cut in half

*4 Rock Cornish hens (about 1½ pounds
    each) or 2 whole pheasants (about
    2 pounds each)*

¼ cup vegetable oil

1 teaspoon garlic salt

Sour Cherry Sauce (right)

Heat oven to 350°. Place lemon half in each
hen cavity. Place hens, breast sides up, on rack
in shallow roasting pan; brush with oil and
sprinkle with garlic salt. Roast uncovered about
1 to 1¼ hours or until hens are done. Remove
lemon from cavity. Serve with Sour Cherry
Sauce.

TO COOK PHEASANTS:

Heat oven to 400°. Place a lemon half in each
pheasant cavity. Rub outside of pheasant with
oil; sprinkle with garlic salt. Place pheasants on
their sides in roasting pan; cook 15 minutes.
Turn to other side; cook 15 minutes. Turn
pheasants breast side up and cook 15 to 25
minutes longer, until meat thermometer registers 150°.

Remove lemon from cavity; cut each pheasant
in half lengthwise.

*An idea for a table decoration using a wire duck. (See following
pages for more decorating ideas.)*

Sour Cherry Sauce

¼ cup packed brown sugar

1 tablespoon cornstarch

½ teaspoon dry mustard

¾ cup water

½ cup dried sour cherries

2 tablespoons lemon juice

½ teaspoon grated lemon peel

Mix brown sugar, cornstarch and mustard in
small saucepan; stir in remaining ingredients.
Cook over low heat, stirring constantly, 6 to 8
minutes until thick.

1 cup.

Following pages: *Fall Game Dinner*

Roasted Autumn Vegetables

———◆———

¼ *cup margarine or butter*

1 *tablespoon fresh or 1 teaspoon dried sage leaves*

1 *clove garlic, crushed*

½ *pound Brussels sprouts, cut into halves*

½ *pound parsnips, peeled and cut into 2-inch pieces*

¼ *pound baby carrots, peeled*

1 *small butternut squash, peeled, seeded and cut into 1-inch pieces*

Heat oven to 375°. Melt margarine in small saucepan; stir in sage and garlic. Place vegetables in rectangular pan, 13 × 9 × 2 inches. Pour margarine mixture over vegetables; stir to coat.

Cover; bake 25 to 30 minutes, stirring occasionally, until vegetables are crisp-tender.

Wild Mushroom Risotto

———◆———

Italian Arborio rice has short, fat grains and cooks up tender with a distinctive flavor. When cooking risotto, the rice should absorb liquid slowly to form a creamy mixture of tender kernels that are still slightly chewy.

2 *tablespoons margarine or butter*

1 *small onion, finely chopped (about ¼ cup)*

8 *ounces wild or white mushrooms, sliced*

1 *cup uncooked Arborio or short grain rice*

2 *cups chicken broth*

½ *cup grated Parmesan cheese*

Place margarine, onion and mushrooms in 10-inch skillet; cook over medium-high heat 2 minutes or until onion is softened. Add rice; stir to coat with margarine.

Stir in chicken broth. Heat to boiling; stir once thoroughly and reduce heat to simmer. Cover; cook 20 to 25 minutes or until rice is almost tender and liquid is absorbed. Stir in Parmesan cheese. Let stand covered 5 minutes.

Pumpkin Bread Pudding

Pumpkin Bread Pudding

------◆------

This custardlike bread pudding is a satisfying finish to a hearty meal. Refrigerate any leftovers.

> *3 cups milk*
> *1 cup packed brown sugar*
> *1 teaspoon ground cinnamon*
> *1 teaspoon vanilla*
> *½ teaspoon ground nutmeg*
> *3 eggs*
> *1 can (16 ounces) pumpkin*
> *6 cups bread cubes*
> *½ cup currants*
> *½ cup chopped pecans*
> *16 pecan halves*

Heat oven to 350°. Grease springform pan, 10 × 3 inches. Mix all ingredients except bread cubes, currants and pecans in large bowl until well blended. Stir in bread cubes, currants and chopped pecans. Let mixture stand 10 minutes; spoon into pan. Arrange pecan halves on top of pudding. Bake 50 to 60 minutes until knife inserted in center comes out clean. Let stand 10 minutes; remove side of pan. Serve warm, with cream or ice cream if desired.

Salad with Hot Cider Dressing

------◆------

> *4 slices bacon, diced*
> *½ cup finely chopped onion*
> *1 tablespoon Dijon mustard*
> *½ teaspoon ground cinnamon*
> *¾ cup apple cider*
> *6 cups torn mixed salad greens*

Cook bacon in large skillet until crisp; drain all but 1 tablespoon fat. Add onion; cook and stir over medium heat 3 minutes until onion is softened. Stir in mustard and cinnamon. Slowly add cider; cook and stir 1 minute until blended. Keep dressing warm. Pour over greens just before serving.

Winter

Dinner for a Frosty Night

Choucroute*

Rye and Sourdough Rolls

Winter Fruit Salad with Honey Dressing*

Cranberry-Apple Cobbler*

Beer

Serves 8

Almost nothing is more welcome than coming in out of the cold to the fragrant smells of dinner cooking. This meal is designed to let you enjoy outdoor activities with guests, then return home to serve dinner. Plan on something close to home for the last hour or so before dinner, such as building a snowman in the backyard or going up on your apartment roof to view the winter constellations. This will allow you to pop the Choucroute into the oven and be close at hand to keep an eye on it. It also guarantees a delicious, welcoming smell when you come in to dinner.

THE FINISHING TOUCH

◆ Use a bread board heaped with rye and sourdough rolls as a centerpiece. Twist a bright linen dish towel around the edge to keep rolls in place.

◆ Set out Choucroute and fruit salad buffet-style, using informal pottery dishes and beer mugs.

◆ Place earthenware crocks with different types of mustard around the serving table.

◆ Make a "winter wonderland" by stringing a small strand of tiny white lights through an arrangement of dried weeds or other dried winter flowers. Also place a string of lights on the mantel, along the windowsill or in a large potted plant.

◆ Turn off overhead lights and place white votive candles on the table, mantel and around the room for light. You may wish to turn on a table lamp or two to have a comfortable light level.

Preceding pages: *Dinner For a Frosty Night*

Choucroute

————◆————

Choucroute is a dish from the Alsace-Lorraine area of France. It typically is made with pork, sausages and sauerkraut, reflecting the German influence in the region. This satisfying dish can be prepared before you leave, and refrigerated. About an hour before dinner, put it into the oven to bake.

4 Polish sausages (about ¾ pound)

4 bratwurst sausages (about ¾ pound)

4 boneless pork loin chops, cut in half (about 1½ pounds)

1 cup chopped onion

½ cup dry white wine or apple juice

2 tart red apples, cored and sliced

1 jar (32 ounces) sauerkraut, drained

Heat oven to 350°. Sauté sausages in large skillet, pricking to release fat; drain. Add pork and sauté until brown. Stir in onion and sauté. Mix all ingredients in Dutch oven; cover. Bake 45 to 55 minutes or until pork reaches 160° on meat thermometer, stirring occasionally.

Winter Fruit Salad

with Honey Dressing

————◆————

Make this salad ahead, and drizzle with dressing just before serving. Light, refreshing fruit is a nice contrast to hearty Choucroute.

Honey Dressing (below)

2 tangerines, peeled and sectioned

2 apples, peeled, cored and sliced

2 bananas, peeled and sliced

1 kiwifruit, peeled and sliced

Prepare Honey Dressing. Divide fruit evenly among 8 salad plates; arrange fruit on plates. Drizzle with Honey Dressing.

Honey Dressing

⅓ cup lemon juice

⅓ cup vegetable oil

⅓ cup honey

⅛ teaspoon ground ginger

Shake all ingredients in tightly covered container.

Preceding page: *A plate of Choucroute.*

Cranberry-Apple Cobbler

————◆————

Assemble cobbler when you get home, and let it bake during dinner.

Topping (right)

2 cups packed brown sugar

1 cup chopped pecans, toasted

1 teaspoon ground cinnamon

4 large tart red apples, peeled, cored and sliced

1 package (12 ounces) fresh cranberries, rinsed

Prepare Topping. Heat oven to 400°. Combine all ingredients except Topping in greased 2-quart casserole. Crumble Topping over fruit mixture. Bake 25 to 30 minutes or until topping is golden brown.

Topping

1 cup all-purpose flour

¾ cup sugar

¼ cup margarine or butter, softened

1 egg, beaten

Combine flour and sugar in medium bowl. Cut in margarine using fork or pastry blender; stir in egg.

Cranberry-Apple Cobbler

Fondue Party

Cheddar Fondue with Vegetables*

Veal Sauté with Sauces*

Sourdough Bread

Fruit Salad

Chocolate Fondue with Fresh Fruit*

Hot Coffee and Tea

Serves 10

*F*ondue is fun whenever you serve it, and these fondues will certainly chase away winter blues. A fondue party is an excellent way to introduce people to one another. Dipping, dunking and then losing morsels of food creates a friendly and informal atmosphere, allowing people to relax and get acquainted. If children are invited to the party, give them their own fondue pot, so they can also relax and not worry about adult supervision.

THE FINISHING TOUCH

◆ The fondue pot will be the centerpiece of the table. Place baskets filled with dipping vegetables and bread around the fondue pot. If you are sitting at a rectangular table, you may want to use two fondue pots, one for each half of the table.

◆ Use a homespun-looking tablecloth with cloth napkins, placed in wooden napkin rings, in a solid, contrasting color.

◆ Be sure to use long-handled fondue forks for dipping. They can be purchased inexpensively, or you can borrow them from friends.

◆ If you have them, use fondue plates, which have special divided sections to hold dipping sauces. If you don't have fondue plates, use plain or ironstone plates.

◆ In honor of fondue's Swiss heritage, hand

letter a name card for each guest and add a number on each to represent the guest's numbered Swiss bank account for the evening. In a hat, place separate slips of paper with all the guests' numbers on them. After dinner, pull a number out of the hat, and give the winner Swiss chocolates as a prize.

◆ Swiss tradition has it that a woman who drops her bread in the fondue must kiss every man at the table, while a man who drops his bread in the fondue must buy everyone a bottle of wine. You may want to institute your own amusing regulations for someone who drops a piece of food in the fondue.

Cheddar Fondue with Vegetables

———◆———

1 medium bunch broccoli, cut into flowerets

1 pound baby carrots, peeled

½ pound pea pods

½ pound mushrooms, cut into halves

1 loaf French bread, cut into cubes

¼ cup margarine or butter

¼ cup all-purpose flour

1½ cups beer or chicken broth

1½ pounds Cheddar cheese, shredded

¼ to ½ teaspoon red pepper sauce

Cook broccoli in boiling water 3 minutes or until crisp-tender; drain. Cook carrots and pea pods in boiling water 2 to 3 minutes or until crisp-tender; drain. Cover and refrigerate all vegetables, including mushrooms, until ready to use. Cover bread cubes.

Melt margarine in large heavy saucepan or skillet; stir in flour. Cook mixture over low heat 3 minutes, stirring constantly. Add beer; heat mixture to boiling. Boil 2 to 3 minutes, stirring constantly, until mixture is thick and smooth. Add cheese, 1 cup at a time, stirring over low heat until cheese is melted and mixture is smooth. Stir in red pepper sauce.

Remove cheese mixture to earthenware fondue dish; keep warm over low heat. Spear vegetables and bread cubes with fondue forks; dip and swirl in fondue.

Veal Sauté
with Sauces

————◆————

10 veal cutlets (about 2½ pounds)

2 eggs, slightly beaten

1 tablespoon water

1½ cups dry bread crumbs

½ teaspoon salt

½ teaspoon pepper

½ cup all-purpose flour

¼ cup margarine or butter

¼ cup vegetable oil

Green Sauce (below)

Creamy Tomato Sauce (right)

Pound veal cutlets into ¼ inch thick. Mix eggs and water in small bowl. Mix bread crumbs, salt and pepper in medium bowl. Coat veal with flour. Dip veal into egg mixture; coat with bread crumb mixture. Heat 2 tablespoons margarine and 2 tablespoons oil in large skillet over medium heat until hot. Cook half the cutlets in margarine mixture about 10 minutes, turning once, until done. Remove veal; keep warm. Repeat with remaining margarine, oil and veal. Serve veal cutlets with Green Sauce and Creamy Tomato Sauce.

Green Sauce

2 cups fresh spinach

1 cup fresh parsley

1 cup plain yogurt

½ cup mayonnaise

Place spinach and parsley in blender or food processor; cover and blend or process until smooth. Stir in yogurt and mayonnaise; cover and refrigerate at least 1 hour to blend flavors.

Creamy Tomato Sauce

1 cup mayonnaise

¼ cup chopped fresh tomato

2 tablespoons tomato paste

1 tablespoon half-and-half

Combine all ingredients. Cover and refrigerate 1 hour or until chilled.

Chocolate Fondue
with Fresh Fruit

————◆————

1 package (12 ounces) semisweet or bittersweet chocolate

1 cup whipping (heavy) cream

¼ cup brandy, cherry liquor or whipping (heavy) cream

1 loaf pound cake (16 ounces), cut into 1-inch cubes

1 pineapple, peeled, cored and cut into cubes

1 pint fresh strawberries, hulled

4 tangerines, peeled and cut into sections

Melt chocolate in medium saucepan over low heat. Stir in whipping cream and brandy; stir until well blended and smooth. Serve in fondue pot or chafing dish, keeping warm over low heat. Dip cake and fruit into chocolate mixture.

Scandinavian Smorgasbord

Herring with Assorted Flat Bread

Assorted Cheeses
(Jarlsberg, Tilsit, Havarti, Gjetost)

Finnish Flat Bread and Rye Bread

Cold Cucumber Salad*

Midnight Sun Salad*

Danish Red Cabbage*

Cold Smoked Salmon with Herb Sauce*

Norwegian Meatballs*

Spiced Ham with Apple Relish*

Spicy Lingonberry Cake*

Swedish Lemon Cream*

———————

Serves 12

*T*he holiday season is a time for parties, and an open house is a friendly, casual way to host a party. It's particularly appealing in this busy season because you prepare the dishes ahead, set the buffet and then are free to enjoy your guests. The informality of a buffet also allows guests to come and go with more flexibility than a sit-down dinner.

THE FINISHING TOUCH

✦ Make handwritten invitations with a Scandinavian rosemaling pattern on the front of the card. You can find books with rosemaling patterns to trace at the library.

✦ Place an evergreen wreath tied with red ribbon on the front door. Print *Velkommen* ("Welcome") on the ribbon.

✦ Decorate the house lavishly with evergreen boughs and twigs. Place them on the mantle, window sills and banisters.

✦ Tie bundles of wheat with ribbon, and place near your front door.

✦ Wrap pots of white azaleas or forced white bulbs with straw, and tie with blue ribbons to echo Scandinavian color tones. Arrange the pots throughout the house.

✦ Instead of one large centerpiece, place several small, straw reindeer among the trays of food; instead of a tablecloth, use a bright woven runner.

✦ Hang Scandinavian straw ornaments over the table, and use Swedish candleholders if you have them or can borrow some from a friend.

✦ On their way out, give guests a small straw ornament tied with a blue ribbon and a sprig of evergreen.

Top left: *Hand-made invitation with Scandanavian rosemaling;* top right: *Traditional rosemaling pattern;* bottom left: *Straw ornaments for guests.* Opposite: *Assorted Cheeses, Flat Bread and condiments.*

Cold Cucumber Salad

————— ✦ —————

Both this salad and Midnight Sun Salad can be prepared the day before the party.

½ cup sugar

⅓ cup water

1 teaspoon white pepper

½ teaspoon salt

1½ cups cider vinegar

4 large cucumbers, peeled and thinly sliced

¼ cup chopped fresh parsley

Mix sugar, water, white pepper and salt in medium saucepan. Heat mixture over medium-high heat to boiling and boil until sugar is dissolved; remove from heat and cool. Stir in vinegar. Pour mixture over cucumber slices; sprinkle with parsley. Cover and refrigerate until ready to serve.

Midnight Sun Salad

———————◆———————

Light flavors of lemon and dill and the bright yellow and green colors of this salad echo the simple, fresh foods of Scandinavia.

Lemon Vinaigrette (below)

1½ pounds bay scallops, cooked

12 to 14 cups assorted salad greens, about 2 to 3 heads (bibb, Boston, escarole, curly endive)

1 pound mushrooms, sliced

1 large yellow bell pepper, cut into thin strips

2 tablespoons chopped fresh dill weed

Lemon slices

Prepare Lemon Vinaigrette. Toss all ingredients except dill weed and lemon slices. Garnish with dill weed and lemon slices.

Lemon Vinaigrette

¾ cup vegetable or light olive oil

¼ cup lemon juice

2 tablespoons Dijon mustard

1 tablespoon minced shallots

¼ teaspoon salt

Shake all ingredients in tightly covered container.

Preceding pages: *Festive Scandinavian Smorgasbord*

Cold Smoked Salmon with Herb Sauce in parchment paper "dish."

Danish Red Cabbage

———————◆———————

The piquant flavor of red currant jelly stirred into this dish makes it typically Danish. Red cabbage as an accompaniment to pork or roast goose completes a traditional Danish holiday dinner.

¾ cup water

½ cup margarine or butter

⅓ cup white vinegar

1 tablespoon sugar

1 large head red cabbage, finely shredded (about 10 cups)

½ cup red currant jelly

Heat oven to 325°. Mix all ingredients except cabbage and jelly in Dutch oven; cook over low heat until margarine is melted and sugar is dissolved. Stir in cabbage; cover and bake about 1 hour or until cabbage is tender. Stir in jelly until melted.

Cold Smoked Salmon with Herb Sauce

———◆———

If you don't have a platter large enough to hold the salmon comfortably, place it on a large piece of parchment paper. Twist both ends and tie with ribbon to match the colors on your table. (See photo on page 134.)

> *5- to 6-pound whole smoked salmon, smoked trout or whitefish*
>
> *Herb Sauce (below)*

Remove head, tail and fins from salmon. Carefully peel off skin. Place on large platter and serve with Herb Sauce. Garnish with fresh dill weed, watercress and lemons if desired.

Herb Sauce

> *1 cup fresh dill weed*
>
> *1 cup watercress*
>
> *1 cup plain yogurt*
>
> *½ cup mayonnaise*
>
> *1 tablespoon grated lemon peel*
>
> *3 green onions, cut into 1-inch pieces*

Place dill weed, watercress and green onions in food processor; cover and process until minced. Stir in remaining ingredients. Cover and refrigerate at least 1 hour to blend flavors.

1¾ cups.

Norwegian Meatballs

———◆———

Finely ground beef and pork and the combination of spices make these meatballs typically Norwegian. Buy ground beef and pork, then ask the butcher to grind it again—this will give you "finely" ground beef and pork.

> *1¼ pounds lean finely ground beef*
>
> *¾ pound finely ground pork*
>
> *½ cup milk*
>
> *¼ cup dry bread crumbs*
>
> *1 teaspoon ground nutmeg*
>
> *¾ teaspoon ground ginger*
>
> *½ teaspoon ground allspice*
>
> *½ teaspoon salt*
>
> *¼ teaspoon pepper*
>
> *1 small onion, finely chopped (about ¼ cup)*
>
> *1 egg, beaten*

Heat oven to 400°. Mix all ingredients in large bowl. Shape into 1-inch meatballs. Place on ungreased jelly roll pan, 15½ × 10½ × 1 inch. Bake 20 to 25 minutes or until done.

Spiced Ham with Apple Relish

◆————

The ham should be warmed just before serving, but you can make the Apple Relish ahead and reheat it.

1 tablespoon whole cloves

1 tablespoon whole allspice

3- to 4-pound fully cooked boneless smoked ham

Apple Relish (below)

Heat oven to 350°. Place cloves and allspice in blender; cover and blend until finely ground. Press spices onto ham. Wrap ham tightly in aluminum foil; place in baking dish. Bake ham about 1 hour or until meat thermometer registers 140°. Prepare Apple Relish. Serve with Apple Relish.

Apple Relish

2 cups sugar

1 cup chopped dried apricots

1 cup golden raisins

½ cup slivered almonds

¼ cup vinegar

2 tablespoons grated orange peel

4 tart apples, peeled, cored and chopped

Mix all ingredients in large saucepan. Heat to boiling, stirring constantly. Reduce heat to low and simmer 20 to 25 minutes, stirring frequently, until apples are tender and mixture is slightly thickened.

4 cups.

Spicy Lingonberry Cake

◆————

Many Scandinavians are inveterate gatherers of wild berries. Lingonberries, one of the most abundant wild berries, grow wild in forests. They resemble cranberries in flavor and appearance except that they are much smaller and have a slight pinelike flavor. Cardamom seeds can be purchased already hulled. If not, the thin white shell should be removed before using.

3 cups all-purpose flour

2 cups granulated sugar

1½ teaspoons baking powder

½ teaspoon baking soda

1 tablespoon crushed cardamom seeds

1 cup milk

¾ cup margarine or butter, melted

3 eggs

1 cup fresh lingonberries or cranberries

Powdered sugar

Heat oven to 350°. Grease and flour 12-cup bundt cake pan. Mix flour, granulated sugar, baking powder, baking soda and cardamom in large bowl. Add milk, margarine and eggs; beat on medium speed 2 minutes, stirring occasionally. Stir in lingonberries. Spoon mixture into pan. Bake 50 to 60 minutes or until wooden pick inserted in center comes out clean. Cool 10 minutes; remove from pan. Sprinkle with powdered sugar.

Spicy Lingonberry Cake

Swedish Lemon Cream

Swedish Lemon Cream

Lemon Cream is similar to crème fraîche, but it is thickened with gelatin. The delicate, rich flavor complements the other foods in this smorgasbord nicely.

> *2 envelopes unflavored gelatin*
> *¾ cup lemon juice*
> *½ cup boiling water*
> *½ cup sugar*
> *2 tablespoons grated lemon peel*
> *4 cups whipping (heavy) cream*
> *⅓ cup sugar*
> *2 packages (10 ounces each) frozen raspberries in syrup, thawed*

Lightly oil 8-cup mold. Sprinkle gelatin over lemon juice in large bowl to soften. Gradually stir in boiling water until gelatin is dissolved. Stir in ½ cup sugar and the lemon peel.

Beat whipping cream with ⅓ cup sugar until mixture forms soft peaks. Fold lemon mixture into whipped cream. Spoon into mold. Cover and refrigerate 2 hours or until firm. Serve with raspberries.

Christmas Dinner

Strawberry-Kiwifruit-Spinach Salad*

Red Caviar Dip*

Beef Tenderloin with Citrus Béarnaise*

Ricotta-stuffed Potatoes*

Fresh Vegetable Platter

Chocolate Eclair Torte*

Sparkling Catawba Grape Juice

Serves 6

*C*hristmas dinner is one of the year's most festive dinners, and it is the time to pull out all the stops! Every family has traditions they share at this season; our menu builds on traditional elements, and then adds some exciting twists. This dinner can be served as a lunch, in the early afternoon or as the evening meal, whatever suits your schedule.

——— THE FINISHING TOUCH ———

◆ This is a meal in which you have a head start on decorating, as you have already decorated your home for the Christmas season. Build on the decorating themes and motifs in your home to personalize your Christmas table. Included here are decorating ideas for you to incorporate into an existing decorating scheme or to use as new and inventive decorating ideas.

◆ Decorate your home with small boxwood trees trimmed with red peppers, red lilies, red berries and white velvet bows. Place them on tables, the mantelpiece and window ledges, and use one as a centerpiece.

◆ Fill a crystal or glass bowl with pinecones, fresh persimmons, unshelled nuts, holly and red flowers such as roses, lilies, carnations and chrysanthemums as a centerpiece. You can make a second arrangement for your entrance hall or living room.

◆ Display Christmas toys and folk art by making a skating pond centerpiece. Use a small, unframed mirror that fits comfortably in the center of your table. Line the rim of the mirror with cotton to form snow. Place small figures on the mirror as skaters. Surround the "pond" with small red candles. Decorate the dining room with Christmas toys and folk art, such as wooden Santa Claus figures, wind-up Christmas toys, wooden reindeer or other items.

◆ Pick your two favorite Christmas colors—red and green, silver and white or gold and red—and decorate only in those two colors. Buy inexpensive Christmas tree balls in those two colors for your tree, then fill a large, low bowl with extra Christmas tree balls and use as a centerpiece.

◆ After dinner, play a new game, organize a caroling expedition or watch your favorite Christmas movie together.

Strawberry-Kiwifruit-

Spinach Salad

————◆————

1 pint fresh strawberries, cut into halves

2 kiwifruit, peeled and sliced

1 medium bunch fresh spinach, washed and torn into pieces

Dressing (below)

Combine all ingredients in large bowl. Pour dressing over salad just before serving.

Dressing

⅓ cup vegetable oil

2 tablespoons strawberry vinegar

2 tablespoons strawberry jam

Combine all ingredients.

Red Caviar Dip

————◆————

2 tablespoons chopped green onions

1 tablespoon chopped fresh parsley

1 teaspoon lemon juice

1 jar (2 ounces) red caviar

1 container (8 ounces) sour cream (1 cup)

Cut-up fresh vegetables

Mix all ingredients except vegetables in medium bowl. Serve dip with vegetables.

1½ cups.

Beef Tenderloin
with Citrus Béarnaise

———◆———

2- to 3-pound beef tenderloin, trimmed

2 tablespoons dry white wine or white grape juice

1 tablespoon tarragon vinegar

1 tablespoon chopped fresh or 1 teaspoon dried tarragon leaves

3 egg yolks

2 tablespoons orange juice

½ cup butter or margarine, melted

Heat oven to 400°. Place beef on rack in shallow roasting pan. Roast uncovered 30 to 40 minutes until desired doneness.

Mix wine, vinegar and tarragon in small saucepan. Cook over medium-high heat 2 to 3 minutes until slightly reduced. Reduce heat to low. Whisk in egg yolks, one at a time, until well blended. Cook and stir 2 minutes until mixture begins to thicken. Stir in orange juice and melted butter; whisk until smooth. Serve warm over tenderloin.

Ricotta-stuffed
Potatoes

———◆———

These potatoes are a big hit with children!

6 medium baking potatoes, scrubbed

1½ cups ricotta cheese

1 cup grated Parmesan cheese

¼ cup chopped fresh parsley

¼ teaspoon pepper

1 egg, beaten

Heat oven to 375°. Bake potatoes about 1 hour until tender. Cut thin lengthwise slice from each potato; scoop out inside, leaving a thin shell. Mash potatoes in large bowl until no lumps remain. Mix in remaining ingredients; blend well.

Increase oven temperature to 400°. Place shells on ungreased cookie sheet; fill shells with potato mixture. Bake uncovered 20 minutes until filling is hot.

Chocolate Eclair Torte

———◆———

This delicious torte takes the favorite dessert of éclairs and makes it extraspecial for Christmas. Bake pastry the day before serving; wrap tightly. Make custard and chocolate early in the day; assemble torte before serving dinner.

1 cup water
6 tablespoons margarine or butter
1 tablespoon sugar
1 cup all-purpose flour
4 eggs
Custard Filling (right)
Chocolate Sauce (right)
¼ cup sliced almonds

Heat oven to 400°. Grease and flour 2 cookie sheets. Combine water, margarine and sugar in large saucepan; heat to boiling. Stir until margarine is melted; remove from heat. Add flour; beat until smooth. Continue to beat mixture over medium heat about 2 minutes until mixture forms a ball. Cool slightly.

Add eggs, one at a time, beating until well blended. Continue adding eggs and beating until mixture is smooth and shiny. Divide batter evenly between cookie sheets; shape into two 9-inch circles. Bake 15 minutes or until light golden brown. Reduce heat to 350°. Bake 8 minutes; turn oven off and open door. Leave tortes in oven until firm, about 20 minutes. Remove from pan; cool.

To assemble torte, place one baked pastry on large platter. Spoon Custard Filling over pastry; top with remaining pastry. Spoon Chocolate Sauce over torte; garnish with sliced almonds.

Custard Filling

1½ cups milk
½ cup sugar
1 tablespoon all-purpose flour
1 tablespoon cornstarch
½ teaspoon vanilla
2 eggs, beaten
1 cup whipping (heavy) cream, whipped

Scald milk in small saucepan. Beat remaining ingredients except whipped cream in large saucepan. Gradually stir in scalded milk. Cook and stir over medium heat 10 minutes or until mixture thickens. Pour mixture into bowl; cover and refrigerate 1 hour or until well chilled. Fold in whipped cream.

Chocolate Sauce

1 can (5⅓ ounces) evaporated milk
1 package (6 ounces) semisweet chocolate chips (1 cup)
½ cup sugar
2 teaspoons margarine or butter
½ teaspoon vanilla

Heat milk, chocolate chips and sugar to boiling in medium saucepan over medium-high heat. Add margarine and vanilla; stir until margarine is melted.

New Year's Day Brunch

Make-ahead Raisin Brioche*

Strawberry-Orange Juice*

Glazed Canadian Bacon*

Crab and Pepper Hash*

Top Your Own Eggs*

Coffee and Tea

Serves 8

New *Year's Eve is full of fun, and so is the first meal of the year when you serve this eye-opening brunch. So much can be done before, including a special make-ahead brioche, that hosting this brunch doesn't mean rising at dawn, or even particularly early. So celebrate as much as you please the night before, knowing that this brunch can be easily prepared by both early birds and late-night revelers.*

--- **THE FINISHING TOUCH** ---

- ✦ Cover the table with a dark cloth, and sprinkle with white confetti to set a festive tone.
- ✦ Place white flowers in a glass vase as a centerpiece and add glass candlesticks with white candles.
- ✦ Set the table with glass plates and use any

glass serving pieces you may have.

- ✦ Set out a box or basket, ask guests to toss in New Year's resolutions and read them after brunch.
- ✦ Take out photographs of family and guests from the previous year and put them in inexpensive frames. Give them to your

guests as mementos of the past year. Hang some on the wall or prop up on the table as part of the centerpiece.

◆ Put unusual and interesting clocks on the table to show that a new year has started.

◆ Make your own clock by cutting out two circles from construction paper. Paint numbers on the top circle and sprinkle with glitter. Make clock "pop" by wrapping wire around a pencil to make a small spring; remove pencil. Place springs between the circles. (See photo below.)

Make-ahead
Raisin Brioche

◆

1 *package active dry yeast*

3 *tablespoons warm water*

2 *teaspoons sugar*

3½ *cups all-purpose flour*

½ *cup sugar*

1 *teaspoon ground cinnamon*

½ *teaspoon salt*

¾ *cup cold margarine or butter, cut up*

⅓ *cup milk*

3 *eggs*

1½ *cups golden raisins*

1 *egg white, beaten*

Mix yeast, water and 2 teaspoons sugar in small bowl; set aside. Place flour, ½ cup sugar, the cinnamon and salt in food processor fitted with steel blade; cover and process until mixed. Add margarine; process until well blended.

Whisk milk and eggs into yeast mixture; slowly add to flour mixture and process until well blended. Stir in raisins. (Dough will be sticky.) Turn dough out onto well-floured surface. Knead 1 minute until dough is smooth, adding more flour if necessary. Place in large greased bowl; cover tightly. Let dough rise in warm place 40 minutes.

Grease 12 large muffin cups, 3½ × 1½ inches. Punch dough down. Using about ¼ cup dough each, make 12 balls; place in muffin cups. Using about 1 tablespoon dough each, make 12 smaller balls; place on top of each large ball. Cover and refrigerate overnight.

Remove rolls from refrigerator. Let rise in warm place 40 to 45 minutes or until almost double in size. Heat oven to 350°. Uncover; brush rolls with beaten egg white. Bake 22 to 26 minutes until golden brown.

12 brioches.

Detail of clock centerpiece (see directions above).

Strawberry-Orange Juice

———◆———

8 cups orange juice

1 package (10 ounces) frozen sliced strawberries, thawed

Combine orange juice and strawberries in large pitcher until well blended.

Glazed Canadian Bacon

———◆———

¼ cup packed brown sugar

1 tablespoon Dijon mustard

1 pound unsliced Canadian bacon

Heat oven to 350°. Mix brown sugar and mustard in small bowl; spoon over bacon. Bake uncovered 20 to 25 minutes, basting several times with glaze, until meat thermometer registers 140°. Cut into thin slices.

Make-ahead Raisin Brioche with coffee and a basket of New Year's Resolutions.
Opposite: *New Year's Day Brunch*

Crab and Pepper Hash with Strawberry-Orange Juice.

Crab and Pepper Hash

◆

¼ *cup margarine or butter*

¼ *cup chopped green onions (with tops)*

1 *large red bell pepper, chopped*

2 *cloves garlic, crushed*

1½ *pounds small red potatoes, cooked, cut into fourths*

½ *teaspoon salt*

½ *teaspoon pepper*

1 *package (12 ounces) frozen crabmeat, thawed, drained and cartilage removed or salad-style imitation crabmeat, thawed*

Heat margarine in 10-inch skillet until melted. Cook onion, bell pepper and garlic in margarine over medium heat until pepper is tender. Stir in remaining ingredients; cook about 5 minutes, stirring frequently, until hot.

Top Your Own Eggs

◆

½ *cup milk*

¼ *teaspoon pepper*

10 *eggs*

¼ *cup margarine or butter*

Shredded Cheddar cheese

Sour cream

Chopped green chilies

Chopped fresh tomatoes

Place milk, pepper and eggs in blender; cover and blend until mixture is foamy. Heat margarine in 10-inch skillet over medium heat; pour egg mixture into skillet.

As mixture begins to set at bottom and side, gently lift cooked portions with spatula so uncooked portions can flow to bottom. Cook 3 to 5 minutes· or until eggs are thickened throughout but still moist. Serve eggs with cheese, sour cream, green chilies and tomatoes.

Before-the-Slopes Breakfast

Oatmeal Pancakes with Strawberry Sauce*

Herb Sausage*

Oven Hash Browns*

Citrus-Banana Compote*

Coffee and Tea

Serves 6

Hitting the slopes requires a good breakfast, to give you plenty of fuel to last through the morning. The oatmeal pancakes and hash browns have "stick-to-the-ribs" staying power, and the fruit compote will also add energy to the morning. Of course, this breakfast is just as welcome before other cold weather activities such as sledding, skating or museum hopping.

--- THE FINISHING TOUCH ---

◆ Fill a small wooden crate or box with potted plants that are predominantly green, and use as a centerpiece. Place a few patterned wool mittens around the centerpiece.

◆ Set the table with a cheerful blue and white checked cloth, with blue napkins. Or try a red and white checked cloth with red napkins.

◆ Use colorful mittens as trivets—a great use for mittens without mates.

◆ Set out blue dishes (for blue tablecloth) or red dishes (for red tablecloth).

◆ For a ski breakfast, send out invitations from "the Ski Patrol" in the form of a lift ticket.

◆ For a day of museum hopping, send out invitations written on postcards of a work of art in one of the museums you will be visiting.

Oatmeal Pancakes with Strawberry Sauce

————◆————

1 cup quick-cooking oats
3½ cups milk
2 cups all-purpose flour
¼ cup margarine or butter, melted
3 tablespoons sugar
1 tablespoon baking powder
2 eggs
Strawberry Sauce (below)

Mix oats and milk in large bowl; let stand 5 minutes. Add remaining ingredients except Strawberry Sauce. Beat mixture on medium speed until well blended.

Grease griddle with margarine if necessary. For each pancake, pour 3 tablespoons butter onto hot griddle. Cook pancakes until puffed and dry around edges. Turn and cook other side until golden brown. Serve with warm Strawberry Sauce.

About 42 pancakes.

Strawberry Sauce

1 package (10 ounces) frozen sliced strawberries, thawed
2 teaspoons cornstarch

Drain strawberries; reserve liquid. Combine liquid and cornstarch in small saucepan. Cook over medium heat about 1 minute or until mixture boils. Stir in strawberries; cook 1 minute.

Herb Sausage

————◆————

1 pound ground pork
½ pound ground veal
¼ cup chopped fresh parsley
2 tablespoons chopped fresh or 2 teaspoons dried thyme leaves
1 tablespoon chopped fresh or 1 teaspoon dried sage leaves
1 teaspoon salt
½ teaspoon pepper
4 green onions (with tops), finely chopped
1 tablespoon vegetable oil

Mix all ingredients except oil in large bowl until well blended. Form mixture into 18 balls; flatten into patties ½ inch thick.

Heat oil in large skillet. Cook patties over medium heat 4 to 5 minutes on each side until brown and no longer pink inside; drain.

Oven Hash Browns

———————◆———————

Put the hash browns in the oven and bake while preparing the pancakes.

2 pounds baking potatoes (about 5 medium), peeled and shredded

½ cup finely chopped onion

1 teaspoon salt

½ teaspoon pepper

2 tablespoons margarine or butter, melted

2 tablespoons vegetable oil

Heat oven to 400°. Toss potatoes with onion, salt and pepper in large bowl. Pour margarine and oil into rectangular pan, 13 × 9 × 2 inches; add potato mixture. Bake 20 to 25 minutes, turning once, until golden brown.

Citrus-Banana Compote

———————◆———————

½ cup sugar

½ cup water

2 tablespoons grated orange peel

2 tablespoons grated lime peel

4 bananas, peeled and sliced

2 oranges, peeled and cut into sections

2 tablespoons lime juice

Heat sugar and water to boiling in small saucepan over medium heat. Stir in orange peel and lime peel; boil 2 minutes, stirring occasionally. Let mixture stand 5 minutes.

Mix bananas and oranges with lime juice in medium bowl. Pour warm syrup over fruit. Serve fruit warm.

Cozy Winter Lunch

Vegetable—Cheddar Cheese Soup*

Apple-Buckwheat Muffins*

Chicken Tortellini Soup*

Winter Coleslaw*

Sour Cream—Raisin Bars*

Hot and Cold Cider

Serves 8

Cold winter days are brightened by a cozy lunch, either by the fireplace or close to a toasty radiator. This lunch is just right before setting out for an afternoon of winter sports—cross-country skiing, skating, snowball fighting, sledding or other hearty outdoor activity.

THE FINISHING TOUCH

- Decorate the table with birch branches or evergreen boughs. Fill a rustic birch or twig basket with winter fruit and wild berries to use as a centerpiece and surround with pieces of curled birchbark. You may want to serve this lunch from a low table in front of the fireplace, in buffet form, rather than as a sit-down lunch. In that case, use the basket as a focal point and place the branches or boughs around the room.
- Fill a basket, or baskets, with plastic balls that have been lightly sprayed with artificial snow. Tuck a few pinecones into the basket as well.

- Use old skis, skates, sleds or other athletic equipment to decorate the dining room.
- Put a black and white striped cloth or washable Hudson Bay blanket on the table, with red cloth napkins.
- Set the table with red mugs, and red and black plaid or checked dishes. You can also use other bright primary colors that harmonize with your tablecloth and napkins.
- Round up extra gloves, mittens, scarves and hats, place in a basket next to the door and let guests help themselves.
- Wrap up leftover Sour Cream—Raisin Bars and bring along for a snack in the afternoon.

Cozy Winter Lunch served, by the fire.

Vegetable–Cheddar Cheese Soup

———◆———

½ cup margarine or butter

1 cup finely chopped carrot

½ cup finely chopped onion

½ cup finely chopped celery

2 medium zucchini, cut into 2-inch strips

½ cup all-purpose flour

1 teaspoon dry mustard

2 cups chicken broth

2 cups half-and-half

3 cups shredded Cheddar cheese

Heat margarine in Dutch oven until melted. Cook carrot, onion and celery in margarine until softened. Stir in zucchini and cook about 2 minutes or until crisp-tender. Mix flour and mustard; stir into vegetable mixture. Gradually stir in chicken broth and half-and-half. Cook over medium heat, stirring constantly until mixture boils; boil 1 minute. Slowly stir in cheese until melted.

Apple-Buckwheat Muffins

———◆———

Pop muffins in the oven when your first guests arrive, so you can serve them piping hot with soups.

1½ cups all-purpose flour

½ cup buckwheat or whole wheat flour

½ cup sugar

1 tablespoon baking powder

¼ teaspoon salt

¾ cup apple juice

¼ cup margarine or butter, melted

1 egg

1 cup chopped walnuts

1 large tart apple, peeled, cored and chopped

Heat oven to 400°. Grease bottoms only of 18 medium muffin cups or line with paper baking cups. Mix all-purpose flour, buckwheat flour, sugar, baking powder and salt in large bowl. Stir in apple juice, margarine and egg just until blended (batter will be lumpy). Stir in walnuts and chopped apple. Divide batter evenly among muffin cups, filling two-thirds full. Bake 20 to 25 minutes or until wooden pick inserted in center comes out clean. Cool 5 minutes; remove from pan.

18 muffins.

Chicken Tortellini Soup with Apple-Buckwheat Muffins.

Chicken Tortellini Soup

———◆———

¼ cup margarine or butter

½ cup finely chopped onion

½ cup finely chopped celery

4 skinless boneless chicken breast halves, cut into 1-inch pieces (about 1½ pounds)

¼ cup all-purpose flour

½ teaspoon pepper

4½ cups chicken broth

1 package (16 ounces) cheese-filled tortellini, cooked

Parmesan cheese

Heat margarine in large saucepan until melted. Cook and stir onion, celery and chicken in margarine over medium heat about 8 minutes or until chicken is done. Stir in flour and pepper; gradually add chicken broth. Cook over medium heat, stirring constantly until mixture boils; boil 1 minute. Stir in tortellini; heat until warm. Serve with Parmesan cheese.

Winter Coleslaw

———◆———

You can make this coleslaw the night before and the Oriental flavors of sesame and ginger will be more pronounced.

⅓ cup vegetable oil

¼ cup rice wine vinegar

2 tablespoons sesame oil

½ teaspoon ground ginger

1 cup sliced almonds, toasted

¼ cup thinly sliced green onions (with tops)

1 small head green cabbage, shredded (about 6 cups)

1 can (8 ounces) sliced water chestnuts, drained

1 can (11 ounces) mandarin orange segments, drained

Mix vegetable oil, vinegar, sesame oil, and ginger in small bowl. Combine remaining ingredients in large bowl; toss with vinegar mixture. Cover and refrigerate at least 1 hour to blend flavors.

Sour Cream–Raisin Bars

————◆————

These bars are another good make-ahead item. Also, the raisins in these bars are a good source of energy—great for strenuous outdoor activities.

2 cups raisins

1 cup margarine or butter

1 cup packed brown sugar

2 cups quick-cooking oats

1½ cups all-purpose flour

1 teaspoon baking soda

1 cup sour cream

¾ cup granulated sugar

2 tablespoons all-purpose flour

1 tablespoon grated lemon peel

1 teaspoon vanilla

1 egg

Heat oven to 350°. Place raisins in medium saucepan; add water to cover raisins. Cook raisins over medium heat 5 minutes or until softened; drain. Set aside.

Blend together margarine and brown sugar in large bowl. Add oats, 1½ cups flour and the baking soda. Pat half of the mixture into bottom of rectangular pan, 13 × 9 × 2 inches. Bake 10 to 12 minutes or until golden brown.

Combine raisins with remaining ingredients except brown sugar mixture in large bowl; mix well. Pour over baked crust. Crumble remaining brown sugar mixture over filling. Bake 25 to 30 minutes or until top is golden brown and filling is set.

32 bars.

Hot cider with cinnamon sticks.

Valentine's Day Dinner for Two

Garlic Rösti Potatoes*

Lamb Chops with Marsala Sauce*

Broccoli with Pine Nuts*

Coeur à la Crème with Berries*

Wine

Serves 2

Valentine's Day is the perfect night to serve a dinner for just the two of you. Clear your calendar, unplug the phone and indulge yourselves. If both of you enjoy cooking, make this meal together. You can also prepare everything ahead, and broil the chops and potatoes just before serving.

——— THE FINISHING TOUCH ———

- Make a nosegay of red miniature carnations and pink rosebuds, add a few red paper streamers and wrap it in white lace paper. Place the nosegay in a tall, stemmed glass. Sprinkle a few candy hearts around the glass.
- Put a white or cream lace tablecloth on a small table for two; you may want to use a table other than your dining room table. Place the table next to the fireplace, by a window with a beautiful view or in some other attractive spot.

- Cut out heart-shaped napkins from pink paper napkins, and decorate them with silver paper arrows.
- Color ice cubes with a drop of red food coloring.
- Served heart-shaped chocolates or cookies with dessert.
- Turn off the lights, and place candles on the table and around the room.
- Play your favorite romantic music.
- Decorate the house with red and pink helium balloons.

Garlic Rösti
Potatoes

———◆———

1¼ pounds boiling potatoes, peeled

2 tablespoons finely chopped onion

2 tablespoons finely chopped fresh parsley

2 cloves garlic, crushed

4 tablespoons margarine or butter

½ cup shredded Gruyère cheese

Cover potatoes with cold water in large saucepan. Heat to boiling; reduce heat and simmer potatoes 10 minutes until just tender. Drain and let cool.

Grate potatoes to make about 4 cups. Blend in onion, parsley and garlic. Melt 2 tablespoons margarine in 10-inch skillet. Add potato mixture; shape in patty. Cook over medium high heat 7 minutes; turn potato onto heatproof platter. Melt remaining 2 tablespoons margarine in skillet. Turn patty into skillet so uncooked side is down; cook 7 minutes until potato is golden brown.

Turn potato patty onto heatproof platter. Sprinkle with shredded cheese. Place under broiler about 1 minute until cheese is melted.

Lamb Chops
with Marsala Sauce

———◆———

2 loin lamb chops (about 1½ inches thick)

1 tablespoon margarine or butter

2 teaspoons cornstarch

½ cup chicken broth

1 tablespoon marsala wine or apple juice

Set oven control to broil. Place lamb on rack in broiler pan. Broil 4 inches from heat 12 to 14 minutes, turning after 6 minutes, until brown; keep warm.

Melt margarine in small saucepan; whisk in cornstarch until smooth. Stir in broth and wine; cook over low heat 2 to 3 minutes, stirring frequently, until it thickens slightly. Spoon sauce over lamb.

Broccoli with Pine Nuts

———◆———

¾ pound fresh broccoli, cut into spears
¼ cup margarine or butter
½ cup pine nuts

Heat 1 cup water to boiling in medium saucepan; add broccoli. Cook about 10 minutes until stems are crisp-tender; drain. Melt margarine in 8-inch skillet; add pine nuts. Cook over medium heat 5 minutes until nuts are golden brown, stirring frequently. Combine nuts and broccoli.

Coeur à la Crème

with Berries

———◆———

This dessert is even better when made the day before. Garnish with berries just before serving.

½ cup sour cream
¼ cup sugar
1 tablespoon grated lemon peel
1 package (8 ounces) cream cheese
1 cup whipping (heavy) cream, whipped
1 cup strawberries, halved

Line a 3-cup heart mold with cheesecloth. Mix all ingredients except whipped cream and berries until smooth. Fold in whipped cream. Spoon mixture into mold; cover and refrigerate 6 hours. Uncover cheese and invert onto serving plate; remove cheesecloth. Garnish with berries.

METRIC CONVERSION GUIDE

U.S. UNITS	CANADIAN METRIC	AUSTRALIAN METRIC
Volume		
1/4 teaspoon	1 mL	1 ml
1/2 teaspoon	2 mL	2 ml
1 teaspoon	5 mL	5 ml
1 tablespoon	15 mL	20 ml
1/4 cup	50 mL	60 ml
1/3 cup	75 mL	80 ml
1/2 cup	125 mL	125 ml
2/3 cup	150 mL	170 ml
3/4 cup	175 mL	190 ml
1 cup	250 mL	250 ml
1 quart	1 liter	1 liter
1 1/2 quarts	1.5 liter	1.5 liter
2 quarts	2 liters	2 liters
2 1/2 quarts	2.5 liters	2.5 liters
3 quarts	3 liters	3 liters
4 quarts	4 liters	4 liters
Weight		
1 ounce	30 grams	30 grams
2 ounces	55 grams	60 grams
3 ounces	85 grams	90 grams
4 ounces (1/4 pound)	115 grams	125 grams
8 ounces (1/2 pound)	225 grams	225 grams
16 ounces (1 pound)	455 grams	500 grams
1 pound	455 grams	1/2 kilogram

Measurements		**Temperatures**	
Inches	Centimeters	Fahrenheit	Celsius
1	2.5	32°	0°
2	5.0	212°	100°
3	7.5	250°	120°
4	10.0	275°	140°
5	12.5	300°	150°
6	15.0	325°	160°
7	17.5	350°	180°
8	20.5	375°	190°
9	23.0	400°	200°
10	25.5	425°	220°
11	28.0	450°	230°
12	30.5	475°	240°
13	33.0	500°	260°
14	35.5		
15	38.0		

NOTE

The recipes in this cookbook have not been developed or tested using metric measures. When converting recipes to metric, some variations in quality may be noted.

Index

GENERAL MILLS, INC.

Managing Editor: Lois Tlusty
Director, Betty Crocker Food and Publications Center: Marcia Copeland
Food Stylists: Cindy Lund, Mary Sethre, Kate Courtney Condon
Photographer: Nanci Doonan Dixon
Photography Assistants: Scott Wyberg and Chuck Carver

PRENTICE HALL

Publisher: Nina D. Hoffman
Vice President and Editor-in-Chief: Gerard Helferich
Executive Editor: Rebecca W. Atwater
Editor: Anne Ficklen
Assistant Editor: Rachel Simon
Senior Production Manager: Susan Joseph
Photographic Director: Carmen Bonilla
Propping Assistant: Michael Lowe
Production Editors: Vincent J. Janoski and Kimberly Ann Ebert